"We're expecting a baby. But I never courted you, not in the traditional way. Did you miss that?"

"Sort of, but given our family histories, we didn't have any choice." In truth, she'd mostly been happy sneaking off with him. "How about you?"

"Fantasies kept the relationship alive for me— remembering what really happened between us and imagining more. It's just...we never got to know each other well."

It wasn't until that moment that she also realized they hadn't. Not really. Even now, they tiptoed around each other, testing each other's reactions. "I guess not."

He brushed her hair from her face, then touched her ear, her cheek, her jaw. "I know that you like it when I kiss this spot under your ear."

He leaned forward and did just that, sending shivers through her.

* * *

RED VALLEY RANCHERS:
Brothers who work the land...
side by side with the women they love!

Dear Reader,

An Early Christmas Gift is a story about second chances—a do-over, if you will—except that the second time around comes after years have passed, maturity is achieved and clarity is more possible.

Jenny Ryder and Win Morgan were born into rival cattle-ranching families. A relationship between them seems impossible. But when love is involved, is anything impossible? It takes strength to embark on a forbidden journey with someone, even for love, but sometimes your heart has to dictate your actions no matter what your head says.

I hope you enjoy Jenny and Win's journey. And I wish you the best holiday possible!

Susan

An Early Christmas Gift

—

Susan Crosby

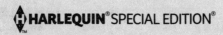
HARLEQUIN® SPECIAL EDITION®

ISBN-13: 978-0-373-65785-8

AN EARLY CHRISTMAS GIFT

Printed in U.S.A.

SUSAN CROSBY

believes in the value of setting goals, but also in the magic of making wishes, which often do come true—as long as she works hard enough. Along life's journey she's done a lot of the usual things—married, had children, attended college a little later than the average coed and earned a B.A. in English. Then she dove off the deep end into a full-time writing career, a wish come true.

Susan enjoys writing about people who take a chance on love, sometimes against all odds. She loves warm, strong heroes and good-hearted, self-reliant heroines, and she will always believe in happily-ever-after.

More can be learned about her at www.susancrosby.com.

For my heroines—Georgia Bockoven,
Robin Burcell and Christine Rimmer—
oustanding writers, generous friends and loving women
Thank you from the top and bottom of my heart.

And with thanks to Gail and David Winslow, creators
and owners of the gorgeous Mt. Shasta Lavender Farms.
Your input was invaluable.

Chapter One

Jenny Ryder's senses heightened as she stepped onto the sidewalk in front of the hundred-year-old building. Anxiety tasted sharp in her mouth. Cars rumbled along Main Street, vibrating under her feet. And the majestic sight of the cloud-covered Gold Ridge Mountain was reflected in the Bank of Red Valley's glass door as she grabbed the cold metal pull. She had an appointment with the bank president, Jacob Campbell, who held her future in his hands.

She felt all grown up in the bank's cool, quiet environment, and was glad she'd dressed like a woman who meant business, not a college student.

Jenny glanced around, not seeing anyone she knew well enough to greet beyond a wave and a smile, even though she'd been born and raised in the small northern California city. She headed straight to Mr. Campbell's office. His assistant greeted Jenny, then led the way to the open door.

The sixtyish man stood and offered his hand. "No pigtails anymore, I see."

"I couldn't if I tried," she said. She'd had her wavy auburn hair cut to a more carefree chin length last week. Wash and wear. She'd save time and energy during what she hoped would be very busy days ahead.

"Have a seat, Jenny."

Her knees almost gave way as she lowered herself into a chair across the desk from him. A folder lay open on top. Even upside down she recognized the request-for-loan document she'd painstakingly filled out. Behind it would be her business plan and a personal plea. Her family's business, Ryder Ranch, had been the bank's first customer a hundred years ago. The relationship had held steady through the economic ups and downs of cattle ranching. That should mean something.

"So, you're the last college graduate of your family. That's quite an accomplishment," Mr. Campbell said.

"Our parents were uncompromising," she said with a smile.

"But you majored in farm management, even though the family business is cattle ranching."

"There wouldn't have been room for me at the ranch, not in any position of consequence." She tried not to fidget but she really wanted to end the small talk and get on with her life.

"I can see how anxious you are," Mr. Campbell said, "so I won't make you wait. The loan committee denied your request. I'm sorry."

She felt as if she'd plunged headlong into a wind tunnel. She saw his mouth moving but couldn't hear the words over the roar in her head. *Denied.* She'd been counting on—

"I wish I could refer you to someone else, Jenny, but I doubt you'll find a bank willing to give a novice a loan. Unless, of course, your father will co-sign, but you indicated you didn't want to ask him. Without collateral and a great deal of experience in the field, no one will want to take that kind of risk. You don't even have an income."

Technically she had collateral. She just couldn't use it. "If I got the loan, I'd have a job," she said, trying to smile. Keeping a tight rein on her emotions, she shook his hand before she escaped. "Thank you for your time, Mr. Campbell. I appreciate it."

"Wish I had a different answer for you."

"Me, too."

Thirty seconds later she was headed out of town, going nowhere in particular. Just *going*.

Win Morgan had heard Jenny Ryder was coming home. He'd checked her college's website for the date of her graduation ceremony—June eighth—and figured she'd be back this week, but he hadn't expected to see her right away.

But there she was, almost burning rubber as she took the main road out of town in her fuel-efficient car, which stuck out like a sore thumb among the abundance of pickup trucks.

Win grimaced as she swerved to avoid a truck pulling away from the curb, but it didn't slow her down. She was upset. Or mad.

Or afraid of something?

She'd always been a little high-strung and a lot stubborn, but four years of college should've settled her some, matured her.

Worried, he got into his truck and followed. He had something important to tell her, had already waited too long to do so. Now was as good a time as any—especially since calling on her at Ryder Ranch was impossible. He was a Morgan, after all, and therefore from the enemy camp, their families rival cattle ranchers for more than 150 years.

A light rain started splattering his windshield as Win scouted the land for signs of her. Hay fields claimed most of the area, except for a grove of trees way off in the distance, at river's edge. Would she have gone there? It seemed unlikely, but there wasn't anywhere else. She would've been kicking up dust if it hadn't been sprinkling, which lessened his odds of tracking her.

As he neared the grove, he spotted her fire-engine-red car headfirst in a ditch. Panic struck, then he saw her pop up and start kicking a tire again and again. "I work *hard,*" she shouted. "Harder than any man."

Her feet went out from under her. She landed with a thud, yelling "Ouch!" then adding a few expletives for good measure.

He made his way toward the ditch. If she'd seen him, she hadn't given any indication of it. "You okay?"

Her eyes went wide. Then she curled her arms over her face and laughed, the tone more manic than humorous. "Great. This is just great. The worst moment of my life, and you're the one who witnesses it. My luck runneth over."

He crouched next to her, eyeing her for injuries. "Are you hurt?"

"Just my pride. And my car." She waved a hand toward the offending vehicle.

Apparently she was blaming the car, not the operator, for the accident. "Why were you driving like a bat outta hell?"

"It doesn't matter." Her shoulders slumped.

He'd rather see her mad than defeated, so he strode away. He heard her scramble to her feet.

"Wait. Please, Win. What about my car?" She hurried after him.

"I'm sure any of your big brothers or your father will come to your rescue." He turned and walked backward, then snapped his fingers. "Oh, yeah. No cell service out here. Well, good luck with that, princess."

She plunked her fists on her hips. Good. He'd made her mad. She was back to being Jenny.

"You must own a satellite phone," she said.

"Must I?" He hadn't imagined wanting her still, not after all this time. The shock of it burst inside him, sending need and pain through every cell, every nerve. He had to fight the desire that had never died.

"Did you follow me?" she asked, narrowing her gaze at him, brushing the rain from her face.

"I wanted to talk to you."

"About what?"

He hesitated. They were already taking one secret to their graves. He couldn't hold tight to his bigger secret, one that affected her, too. Still, he didn't know if he could tell her now. They were both too charged up, even if for different reasons....

Coward.

Damn straight.

"You cut your hair," he said.

She touched it but said nothing as they faced each other like duelists. Then the rain stopped being just a sprinkle and turned into a torrent. He grabbed her hand and pulled her along with him to his truck. The same truck in which they'd slept together for the first time four years ago. How the hell was he supposed to chase that image away?

"Do you have a towel or something?" Jenny asked, shoving her dripping hair from her face and plucking at her white blouse.

A blue bandanna landed in her lap.

"That's all I have. Sorry."

Jenny used it on her face. It smelled like him. Even after all these years, she remembered how he smelled. Tasted. Felt. His brown eyes and hair might be considered ordinary, but there was nothing ordinary about him. He was drop-dead gorgeous, and all man.

And the attraction was still there, sizzling, as if it had happened yesterday. It was why she'd avoided him every time she'd come home on school breaks.

Then she remembered he said he had something to tell her. Her heart pounded. She looked at his left hand. No ring. But maybe that was about to change.

She touched his bare ring finger, then jerked her

hand back. Idiot. She had no claims on him. Why did she think she had the right—

"I haven't gotten married," he said. "Guess you ruined me for anyone else."

She couldn't tell whether that was the truth or he was trying to lighten the moment with sarcasm. "Are you living with someone?"

His brows went up, but he answered, "Six ranch hands in a bunkhouse."

"Are you sleeping with anyone?" Mortified, she shoved her face in her hands. "Forget that. Please. I don't know why I asked."

He seemed amused by her embarrassment. "Well, there's a mouse who seems particularly fond of me." He took the bandanna she tossed back at him and dried his face. "Why are you interested in my love life, Jen?"

"You said you wanted to talk to me. I figured…" She let the words trail. Really, what else could it be, except that he was seeing someone? She made a sound of helplessness. "I could really use a drink about now."

He leaned behind the driver's seat and grabbed a sack. "Your wish is my command," he said, presenting her with the six-pack of beer he'd just bought, bowing slightly, the steering wheel keeping the gesture small.

It made her smile. "Thanks, but no thanks."

He put away the bag. "Well, thanks for the walk

down memory lane, anyway," he said, glancing at her wet shirt.

Just having him look at her made her nipples go hard. She put an arm across her breasts, covering herself, but hiding wouldn't do any good, and she knew it. He would remember what she looked like, the same as she remembered him. Nothing changed the fact that she'd given her virginity to him in a glorious moment, and in this very truck. He'd been patient and tender. They'd spent the summer after he'd graduated from college and she from high school meeting when they could in a private niche among the nearby grove of trees. One summer of stolen moments, of emotions taut and explosive—the thrill of a forbidden union, the shock of loving beyond understanding, at least on her part.

Now here they were, four years later, sitting in his truck, the rain creating a magic curtain around them, making it seem as if they were in a world of their own.

Memories assaulted her right and left. Her hands shook. She crossed her arms.

"Cold?" he asked.

She shook her head. "There's just so much going on in my head, snapshots like they sometimes show on TV, images flashing so quickly you can hardly keep up with them."

"Good or bad?"

"Mostly good. Some painful." She touched her fingers to her lips as if he'd just kissed her.

"I know...." He cupped her face with his hand. He didn't ask permission—maybe he could already see she was willing. He pulled her closer. She expected a gentle kiss, one of remembrance, maybe even a kind of friendship they might have after all this time.

But he groaned as he kissed her, not wasting time with finesse but devouring her, arousing her, reawakening and rekindling what had been. His lips were familiar...yet not. His large, rough, trembling hands roamed over her, unbuttoning her blouse and pants. He maneuvered, shifted and angled their bodies until they were both undressed and in the passenger seat, Jenny on top. She lowered herself onto him.

There was homecoming and welcome, and newness, too. She remembered everything about him—and nothing.

Finally she was draped over him, both of them struggling to breathe, and the rain stopped as quickly as it started. The windows were steamed up from their breath and body heat, but the shield of rain was gone.

She sat up and studied his face. *What are you thinking?* she wanted to ask, knowing she didn't dare, not unless she wanted to know the answer. She didn't. He'd made it clear in his years of silence that he wanted nothing from her anymore. Even before, he'd only wanted sex. Their families were rivals. Their union never was meant to be.

But then he dragged his fingers down her bare body. "Do you ever think—"

"Yes." She kissed him to stop the rest of the question, then they went about getting presentable again. Her hands shook. He brushed them away and buttoned her blouse.

Then he passed her his phone. "I don't have any chains in the truck or I'd try to pull you out of the ditch."

She called her father. He would assess the situation before they decided whether they needed a tow truck.

"You probably shouldn't be here when they arrive," she said to Win.

"I imagine they would think I was just being neighborly. Anyway, if they have caller ID, they already know whose phone you used."

She hadn't thought of that.

He eyed her directly, as if waiting for more from her. "Well. That was an unexpected pleasure," he said as he tucked her hair behind her ear then caressed her earlobe.

"Who would've thought that the next time I saw you, we'd make love," she said. She started to climb out of the truck, but turned back to him. "Wait a minute. You said you wanted to talk to me."

She saw hesitation in his eyes.

"Another time. Welcome home, Jen."

He took off immediately. She watched his truck until she couldn't see it anymore. She refused to give in to the tornado of emotions swirling through her. She also needed to pull herself together before her father arrived, especially if her all-seeing mother tagged along. Jenny had come home a day early, wanting to surprise them. She needed to seem happy and excited.

Except she was mostly confused. Win Morgan wasn't just her first lover. They'd also been married—for a month.

That was *some* history they had. She had to keep that secret forever, along with the fact she'd loved him with all her heart, had told him so every day—even though she'd only been a diversion and a responsibility to him. And that part she didn't want to think about. Even though she did. Every single day.

A line of pickups came up the road a little while later—her father and three of her brothers, all there to help.

She was home. It could only get better from here.

Chapter Two

Even though Jenny had seen most of her family a few days ago for her graduation ceremony, seeing them now, after being denied the loan and having crashed her car and made love with Win, brought tears to her eyes. No one questioned it, assuming she was just happy to be home. Which she was. And wasn't.

Her mother cupped her face and looked into her eyes as the men pondered her car from every angle and the best way to extricate it.

"What's wrong?" Dori Ryder asked, tipping back her straw cowboy hat.

Although Jenny had the Ryder blue eyes, she

looked like her mother, which was a good thing, in Jenny's opinion. "Just feeling emotional."

"You were lucky to escape injury."

"Yes." If her mother wanted to think that, it was fine with Jenny.

Dori put an arm around Jenny's shoulder and walked them closer to the men. "Your father says your call came through on Win Morgan's phone."

"He happened by. He didn't have chains, so he couldn't help."

"Why didn't he stay? What if the clouds had opened up again?"

"He left just before you got here. I told him to go."

"Was he bothering you?"

Jenny narrowly stopped herself from laughing hysterically. "Why would you ask that?"

"You seem particularly agitated."

"I think having my car in a ditch would be reason enough for that."

"Jenny, my sweet," her mother said, "you've been able to go with the flow all your life. Nothing ever shakes you."

"Well, I'm not as young as I used to be."

Dori laughed and pulled Jenny in for a tighter hug. "Twenty-two is old now, is it?"

"It's sixty in horse years."

Her mother grinned. "Have you got a tail hidden

in those...pants? Um, you're not wearing Wranglers? Seriously, Jen, what's going on?"

"Didn't get laundry done before I hit the road."

"Jenny," her father called out. "We're gonna call Tex. We can chain 'er up and pull 'er out, but she's gonna need repairs before you can drive it again. Tex might as well just do the whole job."

"Whatever you think, Dad."

"Dori, why don't you and Jen head on home? You can get the party started. I'll ride with Mitch."

"I'll give you my credit card," Jenny said, stepping forward.

"The hell you will. Tex'll be glad to swap for some beef, as always."

And so it begins.... She would be living at the homestead again, therefore her father would "handle" things for her.

"You're too quiet," her mother said as they drove toward the ranch.

Jenny reacted to the seeming criticism. "Well, Mom, in the past two weeks I wrote three papers, took five final exams, graduated, packed and shipped my belongings, then drove home alone from Arizona in two days. I deserve to be tired."

"And snippy?"

Jenny blew out a breath. She *was* being unreasonable. "I'm sorry. I really am. It's just that until now I've always known what came next for me. At the moment, my future is one giant question mark."

"Really? I had the feeling you had big plans in mind. You and Vaughn always had your heads together, talking business."

"Pipe dreams. The truth is that four years of advanced education, given the job situation here, still means I'll probably be asking if you want fries with that."

"I don't think it'll be that bad. This is farm country. You'll find something."

"Profit margins are too small in the family farms to bring in an outsider." Jenny was done talking about it. "So, did I mess things up by coming home a day early? We could put off my welcome-home party until tomorrow, you know."

"We'll eat an hour later than planned, that's all."

They turned onto the road leading to Ryder Ranch—home. Jenny had been back several times a year, most recently on Valentine's Day for her brother Vaughn's wedding, but this felt different. This time she wouldn't be leaving. Her childhood bedroom awaited her, looking the same as the day she left for college. She would have to report where she was going and when she would be back—not because her parents were tyrants, but because it was the courteous thing to do. Still, it felt like an intrusion into her independence.

Then a thought occurred to her. "Is it hard having me come home after all these years empty nesting, Mom?"

"It's different."

Which was a vague answer. In her selfishness, she hadn't considered her parents, only herself. "I'll find a job and an apartment as soon as I can." Maybe her sister, Haley, would let her stay with her for a while. She lived in town, which would be more fun, anyway.

"Of course you will," Dori said, patting her daughter's knee.

That clinched it. She hadn't even placated Jenny by saying there's no hurry or some other motherly thing.

At the ranch, Dori immediately went into party mode. Jenny was a vegetarian, so a portobello mushroom would be grilled along with the steaks. The side dishes would be diverse and plentiful.

For at least a few hours Jenny didn't have time to fret, especially once her two new sisters-in-law came to help and the conversation got noisy and filled with laughter that didn't stop.

But the moment she saw her brother Vaughn, everything changed.

"I expected a call from you," he said, taking her aside.

"They denied the loan." She held up a hand. "I know. I know. You told me they probably wouldn't take me on."

"So will you ask Dad to cosign?"

She shook her head. "Plan B."

"Which is?"

"When I figure it out, I'll let you know."

Her sister-in-law Annie came up to them. "You haven't announced a job, so I'm wondering if you have one lined up."

"Not yet."

Annie laid a hand on her pregnant belly. "I was hoping you might help me out for a while? It's the start of the summer season for me, and being seven months along as I am, I'm finding some limitations I can't overcome on my own. Even with all the tall bedding boxes instead of in-the-ground planting, I'm doing too much bending and kneeling, and too much lifting and toting."

A glimmer of hope touched Jenny's heart as she waited to hear the rest of what Annie had to say.

"I know that it wouldn't be using your degree in the way you want to," Annie said, "but you helped out at Christmas, and we worked well together, and I thought you had fun, too. I'd pay you."

Hope burst into happiness inside Jenny. "I'd love to!" Annie's organic farm was ideal in Jenny's book. Annie had taken the deserted property and turned it into a business that was growing so fast she almost couldn't keep up with it. "When do I start?"

"Tomorrow?"

Jenny crushed her. "Does this constitute a group hug, with the baby in the middle?" she asked Annie, laughing. "Do you know if you're having a boy or a girl?"

"Don't know and don't care," her brother Mitch said, coming up beside Annie and sliding his arm around her waist. "Did she say yes?"

"Enthusiastically," Annie said. "Austin will be happy, too. My eleven-year-old son would rather be working on the ranch than the farm during his summer vacation. Imagine that. And next Monday is the first farmers' market of the season. If you could help with that, I'd be grateful, maybe even take over for the rest of the season?"

"That would be fun."

The relief in Mitch's eyes told Jenny everything. He'd been worried Annie was doing too much. She probably had been.

Jenny's mood improved after that. She felt wanted and needed. She would have someplace to be every morning and work to do.

Later, after the dishes were done and the company gone, Jenny slipped into her twin bed with the denim bedspread she'd bought while in high school. The photos and posters on the walls were the same. Her yearbooks were stacked on a bookshelf. She'd grown up a lot the summer after graduation, but even that wasn't reflected in the room, not to mention her years of college.

She didn't have to give much thought to why she'd made love with Win today. It was another thing that hadn't changed—she was still in love with him.

And for him it was still just sex.

The more things change, the more they stay the same. Whoever said that couldn't have been more right.

Life on Annie's farm, The Barn Yard, was like a constant family reunion. Jenny's brothers Adam and Brody had moved into the farmhouse when Mitch and Annie got married last October. In exchange for rent, they'd remodeled the kitchen and bathroom then painted every room.

They weren't much on keeping house, but their only other choice would've been to move back into the homestead or the old bunkhouse. At ages twenty-seven and thirty, they were too old to move home, and the bunkhouse had been commandeered by their newest sister-in-law, Vaughn's wife, Karyn, who was overseeing a remodeling of that structure for a new tourist venture for the ranch.

The brothers left the farm early each day to work at the ranch, twenty miles away. Mitch dropped in frequently to make sure his pregnant wife was okay and to do any heavy lifting, often bringing Annie's son with him. And the parents came by, as well.

Win could stop by, if he chose. Something he couldn't do at the ranch. But would he? How could he? she reminded herself. He didn't know she was working at the farm. Just another fantasy, one she wasn't sure she wanted to become reality, anyway.

"Do you mind having so much unannounced company?" Jenny asked Annie as they planted fingerling potatoes and artisan lettuce, mainstays of the farm.

"Not at all. My family wasn't close like yours. For me it's a dream come true. When I first took over the farm, people used to stop by unannounced and I didn't like it, but that's because they wanted to buy my property."

"I remember you telling me that. Shep Morgan, right?" Win's father was one of the orneriest men around. Even Jenny would have found him scary to deal with on her own. "And I think you said Win stopped by sometimes, too?" she asked hopefully.

"And your father and Vaughn," Annie said, shaking back her blond hair. Even though it would only be about seventy degrees at the day's peak, it was easy to work up a sweat working outdoors, especially inside the high tunnel greenhouses, which were much warmer, as sheltered as they were. "But that was before Mitch and I got married. The Morgans know there's no way I'd sell this land now. No reason to stop by."

"How long could you have held on if Mitch hadn't come along?"

"Mitch has made my life a whole lot easier, with much less stress and pressure, but I was starting to succeed on my own."

"He seems to let you run the show here just fine."

"Does he?" Annie smiled. "He has impact on my decisions, because he often brings a different perspective to a situation, and I find that helpful. He doesn't have the same emotional connection to this land that I do, which keeps him clearheaded. But he also amazes me, how he can work all day at the ranch and still help me out here. Austin has learned so much from him, too."

Jenny nudged Annie aside and took over planting the potatoes, which required more bending. "Maybe you could pour us some iced tea and we'll take a little break."

"Okay. Can we talk about Win Morgan?" Annie asked over her shoulder as she walked away.

Jenny jolted a little in surprise, then thought it over. She would love to confide in someone, but should it be Annie?

A few minutes later they were sitting on the porch, hands washed clean of soil, sipping iced tea and eating oatmeal-raisin cookies.

"Why do you want to talk about Win?" Jenny asked.

"Mitch tells me that you used Win's phone to call your dad."

"Only because he stopped to see if I needed help, and I haven't switched to a satellite phone yet."

"He was being a Good Samaritan?"

"That's right. Why?"

"Because almost every time I've seen him, he's asked about you. And at Christmas, you avoided him."

"I've always found Win to be the strong, silent type." Which was not really an answer.

"People tend to romanticize the strong, silent types, but actually they usually have nothing to say," Annie commented. "Win has things to say."

"It sounds as if you like him."

"I do. I think he's a victim of his father's bad press. But I think you like him, too."

Jenny stared into space for a few seconds. "I do."

"But?"

"We had a summer fling that our parents weren't aware of four years ago." She bit into her cookie before she said any more.

"Really? And how was it?"

Jenny smiled. "Everything a girl's first love affair should be."

"Made more exciting because your families would have hit their respective roofs."

"Probably. Until yesterday I hadn't seen him in all that time."

"How was it?"

"Look, Annie, I don't want to put you on the spot by telling you things I don't want you to share with Mitch, and I don't want my brother to know."

"I'd keep your confidences. I have to tell you that Karyn has been curious, too, ever since you avoided Win here at Christmas. She plied me with questions I had no answers for."

Jenny felt as close to her two sisters-in-law, whom she barely knew, as her sister, Haley. "I think we should keep it that way. Nothing can happen between Win and me, you know?"

"Why not?"

"Our families—"

Annie interrupted. "I don't know about Win's family, but yours love you, and they would accept him if he's your choice."

"Accept isn't the same as love and welcome."

"In time it could be that. You've got 150 years of bad blood to get past first."

"Well, that's a snap, don't you think?"

"If you love each other, the fact your last name is Ryder and his is Morgan wouldn't matter."

"Who said anything about love? Lust, sure, but—"

A truck pulled into the driveway, one she would've recognized anywhere.

"Looks like Win has come calling," Annie said. "Are you going to hide?"

She couldn't let her sister-in-law think she was a coward. Nor did she want Win to think he had that kind of power over her. Plus she wanted to see him, so why would she hide?

"Howdy," Win said as he ambled to the porch, looking like the rancher he was, hat to boots.

"Hi, Win," Annie said. "Would you join us for iced tea and cookies?"

Win gave Jenny a quick glance. "I'd be obliged, thanks."

"I'll get another glass. Have a seat. But not in my rocking chair." The screen door slammed behind her.

Win didn't hesitate. He sat on the two-person glider next to Jenny.

"You doin' okay?" he asked.

Tiny tornados whipped through her body. "Yes, thank you."

"I take it your car is in the shop since it's not here in the yard."

"Tex towed it to town. The damage was slight."

"Your folks ask why you used my phone?"

"Of course."

"I'll bet your dad wasn't happy I abandoned you."

"I told him that was my doing, that I made you leave."

He eyed her thoughtfully. "I shouldn't have left, no matter what you said. Thought about it last night a lot. I should've stayed."

Jenny squeezed her hands together until they hurt. She wanted to grab him by the shirt and pull him right to her and kiss him until he passed out from the pure pleasure of it.

"I wouldn't mind kissing you, either," he said, leaning close and whispering.

Annie came out the door, making plenty of noise first. "Here you go," she said, passing Win a glass then holding the plate of cookies toward him.

"Thanks, Annie. You make 'em?"

"I did. I have to hide treats or Adam and Brody will eat them in one day. They haven't figured out where I stash stuff. What brings you here?"

"Food, as usual."

His arm was touching Jenny's. She could even feel the definition of his muscles as he moved his arm up and down with each bite of cookie. He wasn't even trying to keep his distance.

"What do you need?"

"My sister is looking to have a standing order with you, one I could pick up weekly."

"We could probably manage that, Win, although most of my product is going to restaurants and markets now. I'm increasing volume this season, however. Do you know what she wants?"

"Not really."

Annie looked from Win to Jenny and back again and smiled. "Maybe Rose should give me a call, like she did before?"

"I'll tell her."

Annie yawned and stretched. "I need to lie down for a little bit, if you don't mind, Jenny?"

"Of course not. What should I work on next?"

"If you could turn the dirt in the third greenhouse boxes, that'll put us ahead of schedule. Nice to see you, Win."

Win rushed to open the door for her. Jenny took advantage of that to escape from the glider. She headed down the steps and toward the greenhouse.

"Guess I'll see you around," Win said.

What? He wasn't going to follow her? Steal a kiss or two or three?

She marched up to him. "Did you know I was here?"

"Nope." He grinned.

Her heart skipped a beat or four.

"Did you think about me last night?" he asked.

"Not for a minute."

"Liar."

"Egotist."

He laughed, then put two fingers against the

pulse on her neck, which she knew was pounding hard. "You've filled out, Jenny Ryder."

She glanced down at her body. "I put on the freshman fifteen that first year, but I lost that. I think I weigh the same now."

"It's distributed a little differently. You've got muscles, for one thing."

"I worked at a farm lab all four years. It involved a lot of physical labor."

He leaned closer. "Did you think about me last night?" he asked again.

"More than I should have."

"Ah. The truth. Thank you." He pressed a soft, sexy kiss against her lips then backed away. "See you."

"Wait. Win."

"What?"

"You wanted to tell me something. Before."

"Another time," he said, as he had yesterday. He touched the brim of his hat.

She stood and stared until he drove off, her heart still thundering, her body heavy with need.

She didn't want to have another secret affair with him, but there was only so long she could resist him, and it was approaching fast.

Chapter Three

Win looked forward to Mondays and Fridays. He picked up Rose's produce order from Annie—and Jenny—on Fridays and went to town on Mondays for the farmers' market. He could've combined the two events and had Annie bring the produce to the farmers' market, but he didn't ask and she didn't offer, as if she knew what he wanted.

Maybe she did. Maybe Jenny had confided in her, although it seemed unlikely.

Win liked the farmers' market, even though he couldn't get there until about six o'clock, an hour before it closed. He always bought a grilled sausage sandwich and a beer, then sat where he could listen to the live music, groups that changed weekly. He knew most of the families. A lot of the kids he'd grown up with were married now, having babies and working their family farms and ranches—or they'd left and never come back, like his two older brothers. His kid sister hadn't gone to college like the rest of the siblings. She'd graduated from high school the year their mother died, and had stayed on to do all the cooking and cleaning. She claimed she was okay with it, but Win couldn't see how. It was a stifling position.

Now and then Win thought about picking up and leaving, finding work somewhere else, where he might be appreciated. But his ties to Morgan Ranch were hard to break, even the hope that something might change. What was that saying? Hope springs eternal? That was his motto these days.

Farmers' market in Red Valley City was a casual event, with only about ten booths this early in the season, growing to fifteen or so at its peak. It was set up in a good location, with lots of traffic and easy parking. Aside from produce, vendors sold beef jerky, eggs and honey products. Annie's booth overflowed with table flowers, which were big sellers. Win could see all the booths from where he sat eating dinner and enjoying the twang of a country trio's rich harmonies.

This was Annie's second season at the market

and Jenny's first. They worked well as a team. A few women patted Annie's belly and lots of people welcomed Jenny home with hugs. She was beloved in the Red Valley.

Win knew the moment Jenny became aware of him. Every so often, she stared beyond the people milling at the booths, as if looking for something—or someone. Then suddenly she zeroed in, holding his gaze for a few seconds before helping her customer choose a bouquet from a huge bucket. The changes in her were subtle after that—her posture a little straighter, her smile a little brighter, her cheeks a little rosier. He swore he could even see her breath quicken.

Win stayed put, watching, satisfyingly pleased at her reaction. He finished his food, talked with a lot of people who stopped to say hello, but kept his gaze on Jenny. At seven o'clock, the country trio announced their last song. Win wished he could ask Jenny to dance. They'd never danced together.

As soon as the song ended, he moseyed over to the booth and offered to help take it down.

"Mitch will be here any second, but thanks," Annie said. "I had the Kileys save some sausage sandwiches. I'm going to go get them."

"Evenin', Jen," he said as Annie walked toward the food truck.

"Win." She was gathering the empty five-gallon containers that had held the bouquets of flowers, then was pouring all the water into one bucket. They'd sold everything they'd brought.

"Want me to dump that?" he asked.

"Sure. Thanks."

She had tipped the three tables on their sides and was folding the legs when he got back, and they stacked them then started on the canopy, even though Mitch had arrived, joining Annie.

"Son."

Win froze for a second when he heard his father's voice. "Hey, Dad. You remember Jenny Ryder?"

"'Course."

"Hi, Mr. Morgan," she said.

"Could I speak to you?" Shep Morgan asked his son.

"Kinda busy right now."

"I can wait." He wandered away, so he wouldn't have to make small talk, Win figured.

Mitch backed the truck up, bringing it close. For the next few minutes Mitch, Win and Jenny loaded the supplies, not letting Annie lift anything. Knowing his father watched, Win didn't make eye contact with Jenny for longer than a second at a time.

He and Mitch shook hands, then they drove off.

His good mood shattered, Win walked to where his father stood, leaning against a tree trunk in the now empty park.

"Consortin' with the enemy, son?"

"In case you didn't notice, Annie Ryder's seven months pregnant. She shouldn't be hefting stuff around."

"You takin' a liking to that gal?"

"I've come to respect Annie a lot, yes."

"I meant the Ryder girl."

"The Ryders may be your enemy, but they're not mine. If you want to continue this line of interrogation, we can do it at home, Dad." He turned his back on his father, not wanting anyone to observe them arguing in public. "Tomorrow."

His father didn't stop him, but Win figured he was pretty mad at him for walking away. Win was so accustomed to the perpetually angry man that it had little impact on him anymore. His father had never even given him a job title. Win couldn't be called the foreman, because it would mean taking the job from the man who'd held that position for thirty years. The term *herdsman* was almost interchangeable with *foreman,* and Win *could* be called that, which would go a long way toward making him feel as if he had a real place at Morgan Ranch.

Shep wasn't inclined to do that, either.

Life had been hard enough while Win had been growing up, but since his mother died, he and his father only butted heads, rarely agreeing on anything, especially when it came to updating their ranching practices to more modern ways. Win would like to go organic and humane like the Ryders, but it would mean a complete change in how they did business, and change wasn't good for Shep Morgan.

Win wasn't ready to go home. It was still light out, maybe an hour until sunset, so he headed to the grove of trees by the river, his and Jen's secret place. He parked at the end of the dirt road, as close to the trees as he could, then he hiked to the river and sat on a boulder, remembering.

They'd been so young that summer. When he'd left for college she was fourteen, so there hadn't been anything between them. He'd barely been aware of her, just catching glimpses of her at town events, but he hadn't looked twice.

It was different when he'd finally come home for good. He'd spotted her the first day, having lunch at the diner with two girlfriends. Her laugh had gotten to him first as he sat at the counter eating a hamburger and fries. He could easily hear their conversation, which hopped from one subject to the next—boys and movie stars and an upcoming rodeo. Her friends were trying to talk her into competing for rodeo queen, but she wasn't having it. He'd thought she could've won, hands down.

At one point she'd made eye contact, her smile wavering for a few seconds before she flashed him a sassy grin, tossing her long, auburn hair over her shoulders. As much as she appealed, he wasn't about to get caught up in her spell, not even for just a flirtatious second. He'd concentrated on his burger again.

Then her girlfriends left and she strolled up to the counter and leaned an elbow near him.

"I'm so sorry about your mom, Win," she said, as if they'd been old friends forever, her blue gaze meeting his directly.

Even though his mother had died on Christmas, it still felt new and raw. He'd kept a lid on his emotions for months, yet one sentence of sympathy from this teenager had his throat closing. "Thanks."

She didn't leave, didn't even move. Finally she said, "Hey, you want to go to the river and talk?"

He had no interest in talking, but... "About what?"

She shrugged. "Whatever."

"I won't be your rebellion, little girl."

She smiled, slow and sure, as if she knew how attracted he was, and that she could get him to turn somersaults just by asking. "I'm eighteen," she said, "and all grown up, in case you hadn't noticed."

Oh, he'd noticed all right. Most girls looked good in their Wranglers, but she took it up a notch. Her rear was round and high, her legs long. And the white T-shirt she wore clung to grown-up breasts.

She laid a hand on his arm. "I apologize, Win. I'm not trying to tease you. Actually, I was thinking you looked like you needed someone to talk to, a friendly ear. I figure things are pretty hard at your place now without your mom."

"Why would I confide in you?"

"I'm probably the safest person around, don't you think? I couldn't tell anyone about it, since we can't be seen together. I promise it'd be just between you and me."

He thought about it for a few long seconds. "You know where the grove sits by the river, 'bout four miles from town?"

"I do."

"I'll meet you there."

"Okay." She left first.

Win followed a couple minutes later, not really expecting her to show up, thinking she'd only been playing a game with him, but she was there.

They'd talked for hours, about anything and everything. She'd cried for his loss, wrapping her arms around him and holding him tight. It'd been his undoing. He tried not to shed any tears in front of her, but she forced him to, made him give in, then ultimately gave him something else to think about when she kissed him.

She looked stunned for a minute, then came back for more. He carried her to his truck and did his best to keep the experience tender for her. They met several times a week after that....

Then she got pregnant, and they'd married in secret—

Win shoved himself away from the boulder and the memories. He got into his truck and headed home, then straight for the bunkhouse. He'd told his father they could talk tomorrow.

Tomorrow would come too soon as it was.

"I was surprised to see Win in the booth with you," Mitch said as they drove back to The Barn Yard to unload the supplies.

"People are particularly kind to pregnant women," Annie said. "And we do business regularly, you know. I like him."

Mitch glanced past his wife to his sister. "He seems to like you, Jen. At least, he couldn't take his eyes off you."

She sniffed. "I have no control over Win Morgan's eyes."

Mitch laughed. "What's that line about a woman protesting too much?"

"No placards being held up here."

He laid a hand on his wife's thigh, a small gesture that said so much. Jenny yearned for that kind of connection. She crossed her arms and stared at the passing scenery, feeling achingly alone, especially when Annie moved his hand to her belly and held tight.

"I think we've got a soccer player in there," Mitch said.

Jenny could barely breathe. She'd had a baby inside her once, too, a lifetime ago, it seemed. And then lost it. She'd mourned for a long time. Had Win? Neither of them had said a word about it since she got home, although he might have been about to right after they'd made love in his truck and he'd trailed a finger down her naked body. She'd interrupted him, not wanting to deal with it then. But now? Could they talk about it now?

"Are you okay?" Annie asked as they pulled into the yard at the farm.

"Sure." Jenny hopped out. Adam and Brody came out of the farmhouse. Between the four of them, they got everything put away in record time.

It was still light out when Mitch dropped off Jenny at the homestead. Her parents had gone to dinner at a friend's house, but they would probably be home soon. They got up early, so they didn't keep late hours. She wandered through the house, which held so many good memories. The only big change was some remodeling they'd done a few years back, removing the wall between the kitchen and the dining and living rooms, opening up the space, modernizing the kitchen at the same time.

There were four bedrooms downstairs and four

upstairs, including the master bedroom and a guest room. As kids they'd never had to share bedrooms, only bathrooms. It'd been a luxury.

Jenny got into the shower and washed off the day. She felt old. Broken. For years she'd been able to channel her emotions into school and work. Now she was left to face truths without distractions.

It would be so easy to fall into another affair with Win. So easy.

But if she hadn't learned her lesson the first time, what good was the lesson?

Chapter Four

Weeks passed. The sameness of the days started to frustrate Jenny, although she was grateful to be working at Annie's farm and happy to take the load off her now eight-months-pregnant sister-in-law. Every Monday Jenny saw Win at the farmers' market, where he always made himself visible. On Fridays he picked up the produce for his sister. Jenny always left that transaction to Annie.

Jenny's life was nothing like she'd expected for herself when she'd come home, and now she was committed to at least two more months helping Annie.

But not today. Today was the Fourth of July. The

Ryders would host a huge picnic for family, staff and friends, then those who wanted to see the fireworks would pile into trucks and drive into town when it was almost dark. Although the fireworks themselves would be set off at the lake, there was good viewing from downtown.

In the meantime, there was corn to be shucked and potatoes to be cubed and beef patties formed. After the guests arrived bearing even more food, the tables groaned with their weight. Kids played noisily. Someone picked up a guitar or a fiddle now and then and played a tune, either patriotic or Western. Her father, tall and fit like his four sons, presided over the event, a combination emcee and king. Her mother seemed relaxed and busy at the same time, having thrown parties like this for over forty years.

Jenny's newest sister-in-law, Karyn, plopped down in a chair next to Jenny and fanned herself with her hand.

"So this is what picnics at Ryder Ranch are like," she said.

"Enjoying yourself?"

"You bet! Here's a hint, though. Never attempt a three-legged race with a husband who is seven inches taller. He was dragging me along."

"It probably didn't help that you were wearing those boots."

Karyn held out a foot and examined her three-inch heels, or what she considered her work boots because the heels were so low—for her. "The height should've helped in the race, but it didn't. I'm telling you, the movies don't capture small-town America right. This has been amazing."

Jenny had come to adore Karyn, who'd been a personal shopper to the stars before finding Vaughn. She'd changed her whole life for him.

"Where's your sister?" Karyn asked.

"She got forced into working, apparently." Physical therapist Haley lived in a small house in town, near the rehab hospital. "Maybe she'll join us for the fireworks. So, how's the new venture going?" Jenny asked.

"It's right on schedule. The bunkhouse addition will be done in a couple of weeks, and the bunkhouse renovation itself soon after. We can open for business mid-August. A maximum of six guests to start, then ten ultimately. Guess who our first guest will be."

"I can't imagine."

"My number one former client, Gloriana Mac-Beth."

"Seriously? A big movie star like that? Do you think she'll enjoy vacationing on a working cattle ranch? Will she really ride herd with the guys?"

"I'm looking forward to finding out myself. I tried to get her to hold off until fall, because you know what summer's like here, but she seemed intent on being our first guest. If she likes it, she'll spread the word. Couldn't ask for better advertising."

"Mom's looking forward to it, too. She'll be cooking up a storm."

"Adam and Brody also seem excited. They'll be in charge of showing the guests the ropes. And since it won't be full-time, they shouldn't get burned out dealing with picky company."

"Hey, Hollywood," Vaughn called out to his wife. "Pie-eating contest."

Karyn hopped up, full of renewed energy. She grinned at Jenny. "I do love this place. And that man."

Jenny figured Karyn would be pregnant soon, if she wasn't already. Dori Ryder would be in her glory, having more grandchildren to love.

Jenny moseyed over to watch the pie-eating contest. Karyn was loudly rooting Vaughn on. Annie and Mitch stood arm in arm, laughing. Adam and Brody were participating, their dates cheering. Everyone had someone special except Jenny.

The thought put her in a mood for the rest of the day, even as she climbed into her car to go into town, deciding not to ride with anyone in case she and Haley wanted to hang out for a while after. She hadn't been able to spend much time with her sister, and she missed her.

She parked in front of Haley's house, grabbed her chair and walked a few blocks to where everyone agreed to meet. If fireworks couldn't put her in a better mood, she didn't know what could.

She found a place for her chair as she greeted everyone. Before she sat, Annie came up to her.

"I need a big favor," Annie said.

"Sure. What?"

"I just found out tonight—and I don't know why I didn't know this earlier—but Adam and Brody will be moving into the bunkhouse addition when it's ready. Would you feel comfortable— I mean, how would you like to move into the farmhouse when they leave? I know it might be a little scary, all alone out there, just you and the chickens. You could get a dog—"

Jenny threw her arms around Annie. "I've got a dead aim," she said, laughing. "I can protect myself. Yes, yes, yes!"

"You won't need furniture or dishes or anything. I don't want rent. You'd be doing me a big favor."

"I can't promise you forever," Jenny said.

"I'll take what I can get."

There were fireworks going off in Jenny's head as well as the night sky. She would have a place of her own for the first time. She wouldn't have to check in with anyone. Her mom and dad could have their empty nest back, which should make them happy, too. And if she didn't have to pay rent, she could save—

Oh, who was she kidding? She made only enough money to pay for her basic needs, with nothing left over to put in savings. She needed to find a second job. Maybe she could wait tables in the evening. After all, she had nothing else going on. Maybe it would take her ten years to qualify for a loan. The way land was selling these days, the old farm might still be available to buy ten years from now.

Jenny walked back to her car after the show, but Haley's house was still dark. She probably had a hot date. Everyone did, after all, except Jenny.

She climbed into the car. Before she could start the engine, the passenger door opened and Win slid in.

"Hey," he said.

She didn't want to give him any indication of how happy she was to see him. "What do you think you're doing?"

"Sayin' hey."

"You've said it."

"Why've you been avoiding me at Annie's farm?"

Because I want to drag you into the house and make hot, sexy love with you. "Your business is with Annie."

"Not anymore."

"What do you mean?"

"I mean she says you're taking over this week, both at the farm and the market. She's retiring to her rocking chair. Guess she's been ordered not to spend so much time on her feet. Who's gonna help you out?"

"At the moment, everything is manageable for one person."

"How about setup and takedown at the farmers' market?"

"One of my brothers will help." She turned her ignition far enough to power down the windows. "If you're going to propose that you help, let me stop you before you offer. Your dad was angry enough that first night."

"My father's opinion doesn't matter to me. He gave up that right years ago when he forbade me to go to college."

Jenny frowned. "But you went to college."

"Yeah. No thanks to him—or my brothers. They left for college and never came back, so he figured I'd do the same."

"You came back, have been back for years. Why is he holding that against you now?"

"I don't think he'll ever feel secure. My brothers didn't want to be on the ranch anymore. I do—enough to put up with a man who tries to dictate my life."

Jenny considered his words. Her father could

be strict, but he loved her. She'd never had a moment's doubt of that. "How about Rose?"

"He's nicer to my sister. He knows I'll show up and work. But with Rose, she'll have options sometime. Marriage. Her own family. He wouldn't do well without her."

"Do you think he'll ever get married again?"

"I can't think of a woman who'd have him."

"The right woman could soften him." Because he was as tense as guitar strings, she touched his face. "I'm sorry you have to live like this."

He laid his hand over hers. "I don't know why I spill my guts around you."

"Because I'm safe."

A beat passed. "I guess."

"Will you inherit the ranch someday, Win?"

"I have no idea. He's probably cut out my brothers, but maybe he'd give the whole thing to Rose. She hasn't disappointed him."

Jenny smiled. "There's time yet."

He turned his head and pressed a kiss into her palm, then kissed her lips, softly, briefly. "I can't get to the market early enough to help you set up, but I'll help you take it down. Count on it."

He opened the car door and climbed out, not saying another word but walking up the street with that cowboy swagger he had that made her want to chase after him and pull him into the nearest bushes.

She laughed at the idea, then she drove off, giving him a little beep as she passed by.

The homestead was quiet when she got home, but she was still wound up from seeing Win and from learning she could live at the farm. She sat on the front porch in one of the many rockers there. The night was crystal clear and full of stars that seemed to be winking at her, as if to say, "See? I told you life would get better."

She let that happiness blanket her for a while. In a couple of weeks she would start another phase of her life.

Life was sweet, and she was determined to enjoy it.

Chapter Five

Life stunk.

Jenny put away the last of her clothes and dropped into a chair in her new bedroom, exhausted. It was ridiculous. She'd spent two days cleaning the farmhouse after her brothers moved out, then she'd moved in her few personal items today, and now she could barely move. She, the one usually with all the energy. Crazy.

She admitted being a little nervous about living by herself way out in the country, with no neighbor—or brother—within shouting distance. Maybe she would get a dog, after all. A rescue dog who was already trained. Maybe a guard dog with big teeth and a ferocious bark who knew the *sic 'em* command already.

She laughed at herself.

"Jenny?"

"In the bedroom, Annie."

Annie came into the room belly first. She only had two weeks to go now and was showing signs of impatience with her discomfort.

"Mitch and I are taking off, unless you need something else?"

"I'm good, thanks." She made herself get out of the chair. "He's going to drop off more chicken feed later? You said the bins are empty."

"I don't know how it happened, except I have pregnancy brain, I guess. I normally don't slip up like that."

They walked to the front door together then out onto the porch.

"I don't want you to worry about a thing," Jenny said. "You've trained me well."

"We're only a phone call away, anytime, Jen, night or day. Since I'm not being *allowed* to drive anymore, I'll get someone to bring me now and then. I'm going to miss smelling my plants!"

They hugged goodbye. Mitch helped his wife into the truck then came over to Jenny.

"Be honest," he said. "Are you scared?"

"A tiny bit. Annie told me it took her quite a while to figure out what each sound was. I'll get there. Go on, Mitch. I'll be fine. Thanks for all your help."

"You're the one doing us the favor. We couldn't have done this without you." He hugged her, then jogged to the truck.

Work was done for the day. Jenny fixed a glass of iced tea and sat on the porch, watching the chickens peck the ground. They'd had to be trained to be shooed into their pen each night by a person instead of Annie's herding dog, Bo. Sometimes it took a half hour to get them all gathered and shut in. She wasn't in the mood yet for that task, so she went into the kitchen and looked in the refrigerator, knowing her mother had left some meals for her.

Jenny's mouth dropped open. "Some" meals? Her freezer was completely full with individual portions of soups, stews and casseroles, all sure to be vegetarian. There were a couple of packages of steaks, with a note saying, "In case you have carnivore company."

Leave it to Mom to think of everything.

Jenny pulled out a portion of something called vegetarian chili and stuck the container in the microwave. She would add fresh tomatoes, cheese and cilantro when it was done, plus sourdough bread. And of course, there were cookies, several dozen, several kinds.

She carried the bowl to the front porch, missing the company of her parents at dinnertime. She welcomed the independence but not the isolation, she realized. She wanted everything—but on her terms.

Jenny toasted the air with her empty spoon, then went into the yard to shoo the chickens into the coop, one of them giving her a merry chase, but Jenny ultimately the victor. She went inside as it was getting dark and turned on the television. Nothing grabbed her attention. She took two chocolate chip cookies out of a bag and poured herself a glass of milk.

Then she heard a vehicle coming up the driveway. Mitch bringing the chicken feed.

But it wasn't. It was Win. She stood at the screen door, not going outside to greet him, which would be the polite thing to do. She wasn't going to ask him inside, either. Not that she was afraid of him, but she was afraid to be alone with him. It wouldn't take more than a few minutes before they were in bed, there was little doubt of that. While one part of her hungered for that, especially since they'd never made love in the privacy of a bedroom, her logical side won out.

Plus she was exhausted. She really didn't want to deal with him.

"Heard you moved in," Win said.

"Word travels fast," she said.

Win leaned a shoulder against the doorjamb,

contemplating her, enjoying the self-protective wall she'd already put up. "I have one particular bird who works only for me. She reported it."

"How nice for you. I'm not letting you inside, Win."

He had to get it over with. Had to tell her, even seeing how she crossed her arms and glared. He loved when she was belligerent. Always had.

But he'd delayed long enough. "We'll just talk."

"We have never *just talked*."

True. "How about coming out on the porch?"

She sighed. Loudly. "I suppose you'd like some cookies, too?"

"Wouldn't turn 'em down."

"Milk?"

"Just cookies, thanks."

She grabbed a baggie off the kitchen table and almost slammed it against his stomach as she went out the screen door.

"You sure Dori Ryder is your mother? The one who's famous for being a gracious hostess?"

"I didn't invite you. And I'm really tired." She headed straight to the rocking chair, which left the two-person glider or the steps for him. He tried not to laugh, but couldn't help himself.

She finally laughed, too. "I'm sorry, Win. I really, truly am exhausted. Then you caught me off guard."

"What's dragging you down?"

She was silent for a few long seconds, then she rubbed her face. "I'm tired of trying to get my future started and only hitting roadblocks."

"This doesn't seem like a roadblock. It's work in your field. It's a house you don't have to share."

"Oh, never mind. I'm not thinking clearly. Of course I'm happy with how my life is going."

Except she wasn't. He could see that. "What more do you want, Jen?"

She closed her eyes, as if picturing something. "A lavender farm."

She said it so quietly, he wasn't sure he heard her right. "Did you say lavender farm?"

She nodded. "I want to grow the plants, but I also want to have a place for weddings, and a distillery to make my own lavender oil so I can manufacture my own products. Someday I'd like to add a B and B."

"Where would you do this?"

"Do you know the old Carson place, way up the ridge?"

"Sure."

"It used to be a lavender farm, so the irrigation lines are already installed, as well as a drainage system. A lot of the plants have survived, even without tending. Do you remember the view from there?"

"Can't say I do."

"It is spectacular. Gold Ridge Mountain is

straight ahead, the entire valley below it, surrounding it. I can picture rows and rows of different variety plants with a labyrinth in the middle. A gift shop to sell our own products."

"But why lavender?"

"Because it's drought resistant and deer resistant. It's easy care—you cut it back once a year. It smells like heaven. And the blooms come in lots of different colors, from white to deep purple. Plus the heavy-duty labor, the time when I'd be working 24/7, is only for four to five months a year. It gives me the freedom for new projects, especially money-making ones."

"Why did the Carsons fail?"

"Lack of interest. Ms. Carson never married, then she passed away without a will, so the property's been tied up in court for a couple of years. Plus no one in her extended family was really interested. They just want to sell."

"What's stopping you from buying it?"

"Can't qualify for a loan. No experience and no collateral."

"I seem to recall you telling me once that you'd have land of your own when you turned twenty-one."

"I do. All of us kids do. But we can't do anything with it but build our own homes on it. It can't be sold, therefore it can't be collateral. It's Ryder land. Period."

Win thought that over. His father would let him have some Morgan land, but Win would have to buy it. "Wouldn't your father cosign, Jen? Or your brothers? Maybe as a group?"

"I want to do it on my own."

Which came as no surprise. "You know it's the stubborn streak in you that holds you back."

"What does that mean?"

"Since you don't qualify for a loan, why be a martyr about it? If you're so sure you can succeed, why not let people invest in you? Because that's what it would be—an investment in you, not just the property. It sounds like it could work—eventually—but it's going to take a lot of money to get there, and a long time to recoup until you make enough profit to live on. It requires patience, which you don't always have."

She opened her arms wide. "See? And what if I fail? I'd be responsible for people losing money. I can't do that."

"Why would you fail? You're smart, you're hardworking, you seem to have thought it out well."

"I worked on my business plan for six months. Vaughn helped me put it together."

She went on to describe the plan, but Win's mind was whirling. Maybe he could be her solution. He could help her. Then maybe she wouldn't be as angry as he'd been anticipating over what he'd kept from her.

"Listen, Jen, I—"

A truck came up the driveway and parked next to Win's. Every damn time he worked up the nerve to tell her, someone or something thwarted the moment—even himself.

"Looks like someone else has a bird keeping him informed," Win said.

"In this case, chickens," Jenny said with a grin. "He's bringing chicken feed, not checking up on me."

Or perhaps both, Win thought.

"Evenin', Win," Mitch said as he sauntered up to the porch.

"Mitch. How's it goin'? Annie doing all right?"

"She's a little cranky these days. Plus she's goin' through that nesting business women tend to have when their time is near."

Win knew Mitch was more than curious by the looks he gave his sister, who didn't offer any explanation of why Win was there, so he didn't either. "I wouldn't know about that. I could write the book on pregnant cows, however. Come to think of it, they get restless, too, don't they?"

Mitch chuckled. "I wouldn't offer that comparison to Annie if I were you. Want to help me unload the chicken feed?"

"Sure." He went down the stairs.

"You're awfully quiet, Jen," Mitch said.

"Nothing to say."

"I'll alert the press."

"Ha-ha."

Win and Mitch each carried a bag of feed into the barn. They opened and dumped one bag into the feed bin. Neither said a word. Then when they got back to the porch, Mitch sat on the glider, picked up the bag of cookies and pulled out a few, obviously not going anywhere until Win left.

"Nice night for a drive," Mitch said.

"Yep." Win saw the discomfort on Jenny's face and decided to leave. He would refine his plan overnight and come back tomorrow.

He said good-night, then maneuvered his truck around Mitch's and down the driveway. His mood had gone from dread to hope, all because she'd shared her dream with him.

Tomorrow would be a much better day.

Possibly.

Win got his chores done earlier than usual, then he showered and changed and headed to see Jenny, more nervous than he'd been the night before.

She wasn't in the yard or the greenhouses, nor did she come out at the sound of his truck. He knocked on the door. No answer. Her car was parked in the yard, but someone could've picked her up.

Maybe Annie had gone into labor— No, Jenny would have driven herself.

He tried the doorknob. It turned easily. Unlocked? What the hell?

"Jenny?" he called.

He thought he heard a response but wasn't sure. "Jen!"

"Bathroom. Please…"

Please help? Please stay away? He hurried down the short hallway to an open door and spotted her on the floor, draped over the toilet.

He dropped to his knees beside her. "What's wrong?"

"Sick. So sick. The flu. I've felt it coming for days."

"Can you stand?"

She plucked at her T-shirt. Her hair was plastered to her head from sweat. "I need a shower."

Win put the toilet seat down and helped her sit. He turned on the shower, letting the water warm up, then he started to pull her T-shirt over her head.

She batted at his hands. "I can do it."

"It's nothing I haven't seen before. Just recently, in fact." He dragged her shirt up and off, balled it up and tossed it in the sink. "Do you think you're done being sick?"

"I don't see how there's anything left in my stomach."

"Okay." He adjusted the water temperature, then helped her stand. "Hold on to me."

She put both her hands on top of his head. He slid her pajama bottoms down, steadying her as she stepped out of them then climbed into the tub/shower.

"Is the temperature okay?" he asked.

"It's good."

He was afraid she would pass out, so he kept the curtain open a couple of feet, keeping her in sight.

"I'll be all right, Win. I feel better."

"Not goin' anywhere, Jen."

When she closed her eyes to shampoo her hair, he took his fill of her with a freedom he hadn't had before. She had the most perfect body. When he'd told her she'd filled out, he'd meant it. Her breasts were larger than—

He stared at her. Not just larger than that summer long ago, but larger than six weeks ago. Fuller. She'd been on top of him, facing him. He'd had the best view possible.

Six weeks. Could she be—

"Are you pregnant?" he asked.

She came to attention so fast she wobbled. He caught her, his shirtsleeve getting soaked in the process.

"No. Of course not. What makes you think so?"

He cupped a breast, and she winced. "That hurts."

"Since when?"

She just looked confused.

"When was your last period?"

"I—I don't know. I'll have to look on my calendar." Shock crept into her expression.

"Aren't you on the pill?"

"No, I— No."

"Why not? I assumed you were. Surely a college student on your own..."

"Well, I'm not," she snapped.

"Then you should've stopped me in the truck that day. What were you thinking?"

"I don't know. I don't know. I got caught up in the moment. Birth control was the last thing on my mind."

"It should've been first. How could this happen a second time?" He turned off the water and wrapped her in a towel.

"I need to get dressed. Alone." Jenny walked past him and into her bedroom, shutting the door. She grabbed the dresser and held tight.

Pregnant? Could she be? She looked at her calendar. Eight weeks since her last period.

He was right. It was her fault. She should've told him she didn't use birth control. There'd been no need. Would he believe that?

She got dressed by rote, towel dried her hair and fluffed it with her fingers, mindless tasks. Then she went to the bathroom to brush her teeth before heading to the living room to face the consequences of her actions.

He was calm. She didn't know why that bothered her, but it did. She'd rather he be upset or angry or something. But his expression was all smoothed out, and he looked like he'd made a decision for the both of them.

"I fixed you some tea and toast," he said. "Sit on the couch, please."

She did, then he lifted her legs so that she was stretched out. He tucked an afghan over her lap, handed her the mug of tea then moved the coffee table closer so that she could reach the toast.

"I'm sorry," she said. "We don't have to get married, you know."

"You're right about that."

His words crushed her. She loved him. It was going to be hard enough telling the world she was pregnant with Win Morgan's child, but to be unwed, too?

He crossed his arms. "What I've been trying to tell you for weeks is that I never filed the divorce papers. We don't have to get married, because we already are. It's a done deal."

Chapter Six

"What?" Jenny sloshed tea onto the coffee table as she put the mug down. "Why?"

"Why what?"

"Why didn't you file the papers? And why didn't you tell me?" She put her feet on the floor and tried to stand, but dropped back down. "All these years I thought I was free to date, even fall in love. What if I'd gotten married without knowing I wasn't divorced?"

"I would've heard about it and stopped the wedding," he said calmly.

His composure annoyed her. "I can't talk to you right now."

"I'm not going anywhere." He sat next to her

"Go *away,* Win. I can't think with you watching me."

"I found you almost passed out. I'm not leaving you alone. Now you sit there and have your tea and toast, and I'll clean up the bathroom. That's the only *think* time I can give you." He turned on his heel and left the room.

But her mind went blank, numbed by the turn of events.

"Maybe I should have a pregnancy test before we jump to conclusions," she called out to him.

He came into the doorway. "A test will confirm it, but we both know it's unnecessary. We've been down this road before."

"And I miscarried."

Silence dropped between them. She wished he would say something that let her know he'd mourned that loss.

But once again a vehicle came up the driveway, interrupting them at another critical moment. Win went to the front window. "It's Annie."

"Who brought her?"

"Someone in a blue VW bug."

"Karyn. Is she coming in, too?"

"Just dropping Annie off, looks like." He pushed open the screen door. "Good morning."

"Hey. You're here early to pick up your order."

She spotted Jenny sitting on the sofa with her still-uneaten toast in front of her. "Are you all right?"

"Not really." Jenny looked at Win. "I'm going to tell her, okay?"

He nodded, then sat beside her, as a show of support, she figured. Annie found a chair, too.

"What's going on?" she asked.

"I'm pregnant."

Annie's brows went up. She looked at Win. "Yours?"

He nodded. "We've been married for four years."

Her mouth dropped open.

"But I thought we were divorced," Jenny said.

Annie put up her hands. "Can we start at the beginning, please?"

Jenny told most of the story, with Win adding commentary of his own.

"Well," Annie said when they were done. "First things first. Win, if you'll drive me somewhere other than Red Valley City, I'll buy a pregnancy test. I know very few people outside of our immediate community, and if it looks strange for a pregnant woman to buy a test kit, so be it."

"I'm not leaving Jen."

"I'm *fine*. Clearheaded and steady. It's morning sickness, not the flu."

He gave her a direct look. "If you promise to just eat your toast and stay here on the sofa."

She saluted him. What she wanted was a hug, a big, long hug that she could melt into and know everything was going to be okay. The thought of telling her parents—

"So help me, Jen, if you're working in the yard when we get back, I'll..."

"You'll what? Don't hover, Win. Please. Annie worked her farm until yesterday. There's no reason I can't do the same thing."

"Not today. Not unless I'm here. Why don't you just sit at the computer and do research on lavender varieties or something."

She could see that he wouldn't leave unless she promised. And she wanted him to leave so that she could have some time to herself to digest it all. "Okay."

"And you'll eat your toast, too."

She saluted again. Annie laughed and headed to the door.

"Wait a sec, Annie," Jenny said. "Why did you come this morning?"

"Mitch was hovering."

Win's mouth twitched. Jenny laughed.

"Ironic, hmm?" Annie said. "He wasn't getting any work done, because he kept either coming home or calling. So you're supposed to be watching out for me, Jenny." She laughed all the way out the door.

Jenny slid down the couch so that she could

look out the window. As soon as Win's truck got out of sight, she sat back, letting her shoulders, her whole body, relax. She reached for the cold toast, which he hadn't buttered, so it didn't taste too bad.

She had to admit she'd liked how he'd just come in and taken charge this morning, although she should be furious that he hadn't followed through on the divorce. Why hadn't he? Did it mean he loved her and hadn't wanted to give her up? If so, why wouldn't he say so? Why had he left her alone all this time? He could've come to see her.

And men say women are complicated. He was layer upon layer upon layer of complication.

And one hot, sexy man. She'd tried so hard to have a relationship at college. She'd been asked out frequently, and sometimes she went but without any follow-through. So she got a reputation as an ice queen and guys stopped asking, which made life much easier for her. She studied and worked, graduating with honors.

Jenny finished the toast, but didn't want the tea. She curled up on the sofa and closed her eyes.

At least now she knew why she'd been so tired. She would take a nap. Win would be proud of her....

Win came through the front door surprised to see Jenny was still on the couch...sleeping? He crouched next to her. Her breathing was steady.

He wanted to brush her hair away from her face but didn't want to wake her. Then she opened her eyes and focused on him, unsmiling.

"I ate my toast."

"I suspect it's the last time you'll take any orders from me."

She smiled, slow and sexy, at least in his eyes. He held up the pregnancy test kit.

"Is Annie here?" she asked.

"I dropped her off at the homestead. Dori can do the watching over."

Jenny reached for the box. "Did you read the instructions?"

"It suggests using the first morning urine, but we bought two kits, so you can try now. Pretty much you just pee on the stick and wait two minutes."

She went into the bathroom. He paced outside the door, then she called him in. They both turned their backs on the stick and didn't even try to make small talk as they waited. Win held his cell phone, ticking off the time.

"Time's up," he said finally, his stomach a hot ball of nerves.

"You look," she said, breathing hard.

His hands shook a little when he lifted the test. "Pregnant," he said.

She spun around and grabbed his hand, looking for herself. "Okay," she whispered, her voice unsteady. "Now what?"

"Now we tell our parents."

"Tell them what? That I'm pregnant, of course. But also that we're already married? And the circumstances that led to that?"

He took her by the arm and guided her to the living room. "I think we should be honest."

"Why?"

"You'd rather they think we were just sleeping together? We're married."

"Barely."

"Barely counts."

"But telling them that means explaining everything."

"We'll yank off the bandage, Jen. The sting won't last long."

"They're going to blame you. You were twenty-two. I was eighteen."

"And you started it. But I won't tell them that."

She opened her mouth as if to protest, then stopped. "I did kinda."

"Kinda?"

"You didn't try to stop it."

"Hell, no. Why would I?" It wasn't as if it had been a dream come true. He hadn't coveted her for years or anything, but he'd known from that moment in the diner when she'd come up to him that he wanted her something fierce. "So, what do you say? We'll go talk to your parents tonight?"

"Yeah. What about your dad?"

"I think that's best left to me to do."

"Will he be angry?"

No doubt about it, he thought. Not only was she pregnant, but she was a Ryder. "I don't know how he'll react."

"Would he fire you?"

"Not in the peak of summer. Look, Jen, whatever happens, we'll get through it. There's an innocent in all this." He laid a hand on her belly, still flat and hard. "People have gotten together and stayed together for less important reasons."

"When do you want to do it?"

"Tonight. Your parents first, then I'll go tell my dad, get my stuff and move in here with you." He waited for her reaction, but nothing came—until about ten seconds went by, as if she'd awakened from a trance.

"Wait. What? Move in here? Tonight? I've had only one night of independence."

That stung. She didn't expect to—want to—live with him? She planned to be pregnant and married *and* independent? No way. "You think I'm not going to live with my *wife?* As it is, everyone is going to be doing the math and coming to the conclusion that we slept together the first day you got back. You want even more talk because I'm not living with you?"

Her mouth tightened. "I guess not."

"You guess not." He shoved himself off the couch and walked away. He didn't know why he thought it would be easy, that because the decisions were taken out of their hands, she would accept their situation and go with it. Obviously that wasn't the case.

"This was preventable, Jen. If you'd told me you didn't use birth control, we wouldn't be in this spot."

"You should have asked," she said.

"I agree. But I didn't, nor did you, and so the consequence is that you give up your independence. And so do I, by the way."

She'd gone all stoic on him, sitting with her hands folded, chin up and eyes straight ahead. "You're right."

Of course he was right. But he didn't want to be *right*. He wanted to be one half of a partnership. Traditionally the man was the one with the shotgun pointed at him, but she was acting like it was pointed at her, forcing her into marriage—or at least living their marriage publicly.

"Our child isn't going to get talked about," he said. "We were married when it was conceived. No one can say otherwise."

"You're right," she repeated. "I was being selfish. I apologize." She stood. "I have work to do. I have a shipment to get ready for pickup at three o'clock to be taken to San Francisco."

"I'll help."

After a moment she nodded, then she started to walk past him. He caught her, drew her into his arms and held her. She fought him for a couple of seconds, then she tightened her hold and pressed her face into his shoulder.

"We're in this together, Jen," he said.

"Okay."

They spent the rest of the day working side by side and lost in their own thoughts about the conversations ahead of them tonight.

We don't have to get married, you know, she had said. That hurt more than anything, he decided. She'd always said she loved him, even though it had made him uncomfortable to hear those words. Apparently that was no longer the case. So now it would be an uphill battle, and he didn't like battles. But it looked like he was in for a few.

By five o'clock, it felt like the longest day of his life—and there was still more to go.

Chapter Seven

"Do your parents know I'm showing up here with you?" Win asked as they parked in front of the homestead that evening.

Jenny stared at the house, not anxious to go inside. "I said I was bringing someone along, but not who. Listen, I've been thinking about the whole honesty business. I don't think we should tell them about the divorce. Why muddy the waters further?"

"Then they'll have questions about why we kept the marriage a secret all this time. Either way, it isn't good."

"But if we tell them you didn't file the paperwork, they'll be even madder at you. This way, they can be upset at both of us equally."

"No." He put a hand over hers. "Honesty."

"They'll ask you why you didn't file the papers." She'd like to know the reason herself.

He opened his door without answering then was at her door before she could hop down.

"I feel like I need to knock. Isn't that weird?" she whispered. "We're here!" she called out as she opened the door.

Her parents were sitting on the sofa in the living room, holding hands. It took barely a second for them to register who Jenny had brought along. They stood.

"You remember Win," Jenny said, forcing out the words.

Win moved forward and offered his hand to each of them. "Evenin'."

Her parents nodded but said nothing.

"Maybe we could sit down?" Jenny said.

"This is a surprise, seeing you together," her mother said as everyone took their seats. "Are you dating?"

"More than that," Win said, taking over. "We're married."

"The hell you are." Her father shot up, so Win did, too.

"For four years," Jenny said.

"Four—?" Her mother shook her head. "That's

impossible. You wouldn't keep something like that from us."

"She thought we were divorced," Win said.

Jenny saw her father's hands fist. "Let's just sit down and talk, please. All of us," she said. "I'm going to tell you the facts, and then we'll fill in the details."

She looked at Win and was suddenly filled with love—the remembered young love of an eighteen-year-old and a more mature love now. She was sorry he'd been trapped—twice—by her, yet he was taking it like the man he was, a strong, capable, honorable man.

"Win and I had a relationship during the summer before I went to college. I got pregnant." She ignored her mother's gasp and kept talking, the words pouring out. "We got married. Then I miscarried. We filed for divorce, and I went to college. When I came home in June, we slept together again. And now I'm pregnant. And Win never filed the divorce papers, so we're still married."

There. She'd yanked off the bandage. She tried to smile at Win when he wrapped his hand around hers and held tight.

"I know you have questions," Jenny said.

"I don't understand the secrecy," her mother said, hurt in her eyes. "I don't understand why you didn't feel you could talk to us about this."

"We were about to," Win said, "when we lost the baby. We were young and stupid, that's all."

And we didn't talk to each other about what we wanted, Jenny thought, remembering.

"That's where your parents come in," her father said. "We're neither young nor stupid. We would've helped."

"My mother had died," Win said. "I wasn't in a good place. My father would've made things worse."

"It just seemed better to keep it to ourselves," Jenny said. "We still would have if I hadn't gotten pregnant again."

"How far along are you, sweetheart?" Dori asked.

"Six weeks. I'll save you trying to figure it out. It was my first day back."

"Obviously what you have is powerful," her mother said hesitantly, putting a hand on her husband's thigh when he glowered. "What are your plans?"

"I'm telling my father tonight," Win said. "I'll move in with Jen at the farm right after."

"Like hell you will," her father said, more of a growl than anything else.

"There needs to be a ceremony," Dori said, giving her husband a quelling look. "Something public."

"But we're already married," Win said.

"Then a renewal of vows, so your families can take part."

"And her mother can see her daughter get married, as she's always wanted," her father said. "She's dreamed of this for longer than you have, Jen."

Jenny looked at Win. "It sounds reasonable," he said. "As long as it's soon. Very soon."

"I can pull together something nice in a week," Dori said. "A week from tomorrow. Saturday. Here at the homestead."

"And you don't move in with my daughter until then," Jim said.

"Hold on," Jenny said. "You can't—"

Win interrupted, making eye contact with her father. "She's living out there alone, with no neighbor in sight. She's pregnant. She miscarried once before. I need to be there."

"She can move back home for the week," her father said in a tone indicating there would be no further discussion on the matter.

"And during the week, you'll come here for dinner, Win, and we can get to know you," Dori said. "Tomorrow night the family will gather, and you'll announce it to everyone. Please extend the invitation to your father and sister."

"He won't come," Win said.

"Invite him anyway. Tell your sister to come

without him. There can be peace between us, Win," her mother said.

After a moment, he nodded.

"Well," Dori said. "This has been quite an evening. I admit I've wondered for years why you never talked about a boy, Jenny, or brought one home."

"Why didn't you file for the divorce?" her father asked Win, apparently not willing to give up the discussion like her mother was.

Win looked at the floor a minute before he spoke. "I can tell you that I don't honestly know, because that's the closest thing to the truth. I procrastinated, and then procrastinated some more. The only reason I even considered a divorce was for Jen's sake. I believe she would've given up college and stayed here. I didn't want her to."

"So you would've remained married?" Jim asked.

Jenny held her breath.

"She was legally mine. We'd created a child together, which made it even more permanent. Not that these thoughts ran through my head then. I was a confused kid. I just knew I didn't want to get in her way. But I didn't want to give her up, either. In my head, we were married, and that was that."

After a moment, Jim nodded, as if satisfied. "I don't envy you your next conversation."

"Thank you, sir." He stood. "Better to get it done with. I'll be back later."

"I need to get some of my stuff from the farmhouse," Jenny said.

"Your mother and I will take you while Win is gone."

"I'm thinking maybe I should move into the farmhouse for the week," Win said. "I'm sure Annie doesn't like it empty."

"You're probably right."

"I'll call her," Win said, then he shook hands with her father. Her mother gave him a hug, which brought a lump to Jenny's throat.

She followed Win out to the porch.

"Feel better?" he asked.

"You were right. Honest was better. You're okay with having the ceremony?"

"It's a good plan, all around." Win was surprised how much the idea appealed to him. As soon as Dori mentioned it, he'd relaxed. It had signaled her acceptance of the situation. "Did you miss having a ceremony the first time? That quick visit to the chapel in Reno wasn't much for memories."

"I missed having my family there. As for the rest, maybe a little. I'd never wanted anything big or fancy. Saturday will be perfect." She put a hand on his chest. "I wouldn't mind going with you to your dad's, Win."

"I know. It'll be ugly. I don't want you there. See you later."

It was fifteen miles to Morgan Ranch. He thought about the stark difference between the Ryder homestead, which he hadn't been inside until tonight, and his family's home, which paled in comparison. What warmth there'd been had gone cold with his mother's passing. Rose tried her hardest, but their father wasn't open to change, neither structural nor cosmetic.

The front door opened as Win reached the top porch step.

"Where the hell have you been?" his father shouted.

"I left you a message. I was dealing with a personal matter." He walked past his father, saw his sister watching TV. She got up to leave.

"Don't go, Rose. I need to talk to both of you," Win said. "Let me take care of this first." He took the box of produce from the farm into the kitchen, tossed the lettuce into the refrigerator. The rest could wait.

Like Jenny, Win simply recited the facts.

With every sentence, his father's face turned a little harder, a little redder. "So you flat-out lied to me at the farmers' market when I asked if you'd taken a liking to the Ryder girl. And you've been lying for four years."

"Her name is Jenny, not 'the Ryder girl,' and

she's my wife, so technically she's 'the Morgan girl.' Her parents are hosting a party for the family tomorrow night to announce we're having a ceremony to renew our vows next Saturday, family only. You're invited. You, too, Rose."

His shy sister glanced nervously at their father. Her brown eyes were filled with apprehension, her slender body stiff with tension.

"Hell will freeze over before I step one foot in that man's house," his father said. "And you just killed your chance of inheriting any part of my ranch. You'll have a job, but nothing more."

He stalked past Win and went straight to his bedroom at the back of the house, slamming the door behind him.

"That went better than I hoped," Win said to Rose, who smiled uneasily. He hadn't expected to inherit the ranch anyway. "Will you come to the party, Rose? Dad'll be mad if you do, but it sure would be nice to have at least one member of my family there."

"I always liked Jenny. She was very kind to me when Mom died. You know, we'd gone to school together since kindergarten, and while we didn't hang out in the same group, she talked to me like I wasn't a Morgan."

Win laughed at that. "Will you come? I'll pick you up if he won't let you use the truck."

"Okay." She blew out a breath.

He hugged her. "Thanks. It means a lot to me."

"Where will you live?"

"At Annie Ryder's farm. I'll take my belongings with me tonight." The fact he was twenty-six years old and his only belongings were his truck and some clothes seemed almost pathetic, he thought. But then, he did have a sizeable bank account since he hadn't spent his wages on anything costly. He wouldn't be coming to the relationship empty-handed.

"Jenny won't join me at the farm until after the ceremony next weekend."

Rose smiled. "Her dad insisted on that condition, I imagine."

"That would be putting it mildly. Well, I need to get going." He started out the door, anxious to get his things from the bunkhouse, then he turned around. "Make him buy you a car of your own. You've earned it."

"Maybe I will."

"Be brave, Rose. You can't take care of him forever. You deserve a life of your own. And feel free to stop by the farm anytime. You'll always be welcome."

Win went out into the cool night where he could breathe again. The worst was over. Now he could focus on the future. He was going to be a father, a much different one than his own.

Still…he'd wanted to be supported by his father, like Jenny was by her family. It stung more than he wanted to admit, having him stalk off and slam the door.

When Win arrived at the homestead, Jenny and Dori were in the kitchen concocting something. He didn't wait for them to ask how it went but said, "I think Rose may come tomorrow, but my father won't."

After a short silence, Jim asked, "Are you hungry?"

That was it? No more questions? "I could eat."

"The girls are fixing tacos."

"Sounds good."

"Maybe Win would like a tour of the house," her mother said, elbowing Jenny. "I'll finish up here."

Jenny led him through a doorway. "Are you all right?" she asked.

I don't stand to inherit any part of the ranch, but... "Everything's good. Which room's yours?"

She walked him down a hall with a lot of doors. On the hallway walls were paintings of each Ryder child on a horse when they were five or six, he guessed.

"Is this your room?" he asked, spotting a painting of a little cowgirl on a horse, hanging next to a doorway. He knew it was her, not her sister, right away. There was that same wide smile and a look in her eyes that warned of impishness. A red cowboy hat draped down her back.

"My room hasn't changed since high school," she said, as if apologizing.

It did look like a teenager's room, with memorabilia scattered around and posters on the walls. He smiled at one of Cinderella scrubbing the floor with mice around her. "No prince?" he asked.

"I thought that was the most unbelievable part of the story." She shrugged. "We earn our way, not have a prince drop into our lives and take care of us."

Win knew it was going to be an uphill battle with her. She would want to work until she gave birth. She wouldn't be good at putting her feet up at night—or during the day—unless the doctor ordered it. Win wanted to take care of her, be her true prince, not some fantasy from a fairy tale.

He was terrified she would miscarry again, afraid of not only losing the baby, but her, too, if there was no baby to keep them together. She was his. He wouldn't let that change.

"Dinner's ready!" Dori called out.

He was about to take Jenny into his arms for a second, but she said, "I'm starved," and walked past him, leaving him to follow and to face his first dinner with her parents. His in-laws.

That was going to take some getting used to.

Chapter Eight

Even amid the whirlwind ceremony plans, Jenny managed to work the farm. Although she was sick every morning, she was happy working in the gardens and the greenhouses, tasks that soothed her, giving her chaotic thoughts a place to land.

She and her mother had debated about an appropriate dress for the ceremony. Dori wanted her to wear a wedding gown. They compromised on a full-skirted, calf-length dress in ivory silk with lace trim. She wanted to wear boots but her sister-in-law Karyn talked her out of it, loaning Jenny her rhinestone-studded high heels.

A renewal-of-vows ceremony didn't require a

minister or a legal official, so her brother Vaughn volunteered to preside. He'd asked Jenny and Win to write something personal that he could use, but neither of them felt comfortable doing so. They planned a brief ceremony then a small party afterward, with only family attending.

The day of the ceremony Jenny waited in her bedroom for someone to come tell her it was time. She sniffed her bouquet, a combination of blooms from Annie's garden and a few roses from her mother's garden. They weren't having attendants, and her parents wouldn't be walking her down the aisle they'd created in the garden, although she wished someone was going to walk with her. She'd never worn such high heels before. Plus she was nervous beyond measure.

A knock on the door startled her. She opened it to find Win standing there.

"You look beautiful," he said, his gaze admiring. "And tall."

She laughed. "Karyn's shoes. You look quite handsome yourself." He wore a black Western suit, white shirt, plus a new black Stetson. He looked more than handsome. She touched the silver bolo tie at his throat, her wedding gift to him the first time around. She was pleased he wore it now.

"What are you doing here, Win?"

"I figured I'd walk down the aisle with you."

She breathed a sigh of relief. "I was afraid I would trip," she admitted.

He presented his arm to her. She took hold, grateful for his thoughtfulness, especially after she'd been cool to him all week. She wasn't even sure why, except that she'd been trying to come to terms with all the changes in her life. Her dreams of just a couple of months ago had gone up in smoke. She would never have the freedom to start her own farm now, even if she could come up with money.

"Jenny," he said, his voice tender. "Don't be scared. Everything will work out. I promise."

He was such a good man, she thought, and she'd turned his life upside down—and was responsible for turning her own upside down, too. Yet here he was, appeasing her parents and suffering through the unspoken sympathy of every guest in attendance today that his father hadn't bothered to show up, although Rose had.

"Thank you for doing this," she said.

He kissed her forehead, then they walked together out the back door into Dori's beautiful garden and the gathering of family standing there. Everyone smiled at them. After the initial shock, they'd accepted Jenny and Win's news as if it was an everyday occurrence.

Vaughn had scoured the internet and his own fertile mind for appropriate things to say under such unusual circumstances. Jenny and Win had bought matching wedding bands, nothing fancy, and without gemstones, but with some swirls and etching. After they exchanged rings, Vaughn ended the ceremony with, "I pronounce you *still* husband and wife. You may kiss your bride."

Everyone cheered. Win smiled and whispered, "That wasn't so bad, was it?"

She smiled back, then he kissed her in a publicly appropriate way before they were surrounded and hugged and kissed and congratulated. A feast awaited them after that. Jenny filled a plate then went to sit across from her new sister-in-law, Rose. Adam and Brody had been charged with keeping her company, but they'd been helping to grill ribeye steaks.

"May I join you?" Jenny asked.

"Of course. Your mom was just here, entertaining me, and Haley before that. I haven't been abandoned." Rose touched Jenny's hand. "I'm sorry about my dad."

"Me, too. Maybe he'll mellow after the baby comes."

Win sat on the bench next to Jenny, setting his loaded plate on the table. "Enjoying yourself?" he asked his sister, who nodded. Then he said to Jenny, "Rose throws a pretty good party herself for our hands and their families."

"You don't eat beef?" Rose said to Jenny.

"I was in the habit of naming every calf when it was born. By the time I was thirteen, I couldn't... I just couldn't."

Because only family was invited, it wasn't a huge crowd, only fourteen. Music played from outdoor speakers and people danced, but it was all casual, with Vaughn and Karyn's seven-year-old daughter, Cassidy, dancing with almost everyone, wearing sparkly shoes she was so proud of. Vaughn led a toast, the newlyweds cut their cake then opened their gifts. There was no time for a honeymoon, but her parents had gotten them a room in Medford for the night.

Jenny was more than a little anxious to get there. She'd been anticipating their wedding night in a big way, had bought a pink lace nightgown for the occasion. They'd have a real bed....

She wanted it to be special, especially since Win had been forced into marriage because she'd been reckless, because divorced or not, they would've married again because of this baby. He was that kind of man. She wouldn't stop feeling guilty about that for a long time. She loved him. She wanted it to work. But she was afraid he was there and would continue to be there because it was the right thing to do, not because he loved her.

He'd never said so, anyway, even though she'd told him every time she'd seen him that long-ago summer.

So she was counting on the night in the hotel to reconnect with him, to start their marriage the right way. Making love would be the first hopeful step for them.

When the bride and groom went inside to change clothes, their guests gathered in front of the house. They formed two lines, locked hands and created a tunnel from the front door to the truck. Jenny and Win ducked and ran. When they reached the truck, they turned to wave goodbye.

"Oh, no!" Annie called out. "My water just broke."

After being peppered with questions, she admitted to having been in labor since the wedding started, and the contractions were regular and close enough to head to the hospital, especially since it was her second child.

Everyone went, including the newlyweds. As a family they took up the entire waiting room, the joy of the earlier event continuing with excited anticipation. Dori was invited to be in the labor and delivery room, and she came out a couple of times with updates, but the last update came from the new addition as a baby's cries could be heard.

They all jumped up and hugged. More time passed, then Mitch emerged.

"It's a boy. Seven pounds, ten ounces. Twenty inches long. We've named him James Mitchell,

and we'll call him Jamie. Everyone is…perfect."
He hugged his father hard, then everyone else.

"You can be first to see him," Mitch said to
Jenny and Win. "Then you need to get going on
your honeymoon right after."

They followed him down the hall. Annie held a
blanketed bundle, his tiny face peeking out.

Jenny felt a rush of emotion—for the baby she
lost, for her fears about the one she carried, for
happiness for Mitch and Annie. She couldn't articulate
anything, couldn't even manage a "Congratulations"
or "He's beautiful." Tears welled and
a kind of desperation settled in her.

After a moment, Win wrapped an arm around
her and moved her into the hall after saying a quick
goodbye to Annie and his mother-in-law.

He found an empty room a couple of doors
down. "What's going on?"

She sniffled. "It's just been a long day. A lot
to absorb."

"Would you just like to go home? Skip spending
the night in Medford?"

"But—it's our wedding night."

"We wouldn't get there before midnight."

"You don't want to go, Win?"

No, he didn't want to go, but he couldn't tell
her that. He didn't want a romantic, sexy night
with her.…

That wasn't true. He wanted that more than anything, but she'd had the miscarriage right after they'd had sex the last time. The guilt he'd lived with ever since then had been overwhelming. It'd been a particularly passionate session of lovemaking, only a week after they'd married. He couldn't risk that again.

"I just think it's late and we're both tired," he said.

"By home, do you mean the farmhouse?"

"Yeah."

She stared at him until he was ready to squirm. "If that's what you want," she said finally.

"I do. I want to be someplace familiar, not a fancy hotel room."

"Then that's what we'll do," she said, sliding her arms around him. "I don't really care, as long as we're together."

He started to lead her out of the room when Dori appeared. They exchanged glances.

"Overtired," Jenny said. "We're going back to the farm, Mom. I'm sorry about not being able to use your gift of the hotel room, but we're beat."

"You can go another time." She rubbed her daughter's back. "Call me tomorrow."

"I will," Jenny said, her mood lightening.

"She's safe in my hands," Win said to Dori.

"I have no doubt of that." She kissed Win's cheek and left.

The drive to the farm took about forty-five min-

utes. Jenny fell asleep right away. Against her pro-
tests, he carried her and her bag into the house, not
stopping until they reached the bedroom. He sat
her on the bed, then returned to the truck to get his
bag, but didn't go into the room right away, giving
her time to change. When he did finally join her,
he brought her a mug of tea.

It was a stall, the first of probably a few. She
wasn't going to react well to his plans, he thought.
Not when she was dressed to thrill in a pretty pink
gown.

"Thank you." She accepted the mug but set it on
the nightstand, not drinking it. Instead she reached
for him, sliding his bolo down.

He grabbed her hand. "I want to sleep alone,"
he said.

"What? Why?"

"You should get a good night's sleep. I don't
want to disturb you."

"Making love is disturbing me?"

"You know what I mean."

"No, I don't. I really don't. I'm your wife. I want
to sleep in the same bed with you."

Like he didn't? He'd been waiting four years for
that privilege. But what if she miscarried because
of it? How could he live with that a second time?

As Win remained silent, Jenny tried to figure
him out. She thought he'd be as anxious as she to
share a bed finally. Even though he was doing the

right thing, she thought he wanted her still. Had he only gotten carried away and now he was stuck with her?

She didn't think she could live with that. She laid a hand on his chest. "Just for tonight, Win?"

"We're both tired, Jenny."

He couldn't even answer her. Fear wrapped around her. She'd completely misread him. He obviously felt forced. He'd been kind because…well, he was a kind man, and a dutiful one.

"All right, Win. I can accept not making love tonight, but not you sleeping in another bed. We're married. We sleep together. What if I need you during the night?" She felt a tiny bit guilty for playing that card, but she had a feeling if she let him go one night, it would continue, and they would never find accord as husband and wife.

He didn't answer but turned out the lights, stripped down to his briefs and got into bed. They stretched out on their backs, side by side. He stared at the ceiling. She was going to have to woo her own husband.

After a minute Jenny smiled, deciding that kind of role reversal might be kind of fun.

"Night," he said, then rolled onto his side.

She snuggled up behind him, wrapping an arm around his waist. His body went rigid. "Relax," she said. "Nothing's going to happen until you want it to. Go to sleep."

He did. Jenny allowed herself the contentment of being in a real bed with him and holding him before she gave in to slumber, as well. She woke up a few times during the night. They never lost contact with each other. If she rolled to her other side, he spooned behind her, his arm over her stomach. Once, they'd been facing each other, their legs entwined. But they were always touching.

For now she would have to be satisfied with that and let the future take care of itself.

Chapter Nine

Win wasn't in bed when Jenny woke up, but he came through the door a minute later carrying a tray. He'd made breakfast—scrambled eggs and toast.

"I've never cooked much," he said, looking adorable. He hadn't combed his hair or shaved, had pulled on his jeans and a T-shirt that looked like it'd been wadded up in a drawer for a year.

"I need to go to the bathroom first."

"Sure."

He set down the tray. She stopped on her way out of the room to kiss him. "Thank you."

She looked in the bathroom mirror. It was not

a pretty sight, even after she brushed her hair and teeth. She hadn't washed her face last night, and mascara still darkened the skin under her eyes, but she didn't want the eggs to get cold, even though she wasn't sure she could keep food down.

"How'd you sleep?" he asked. He'd brought two forks. They ate off the same plate.

"Good." Better than that, actually. She'd been restless and aware of him, but in a good way. "I liked sleeping with you. Very much."

She was about to move closer to him when her stomach rebelled against the eggs. She jumped out of bed and raced for the bathroom, throwing up everything she'd just eaten. She was aware that Win had followed and was quietly standing nearby, which both comforted and embarrassed her. After she seemed to be done, he wet a washcloth and handed it to her.

"Sorry," she said. "I should've told you the morning sickness hasn't ended yet. Usually I just drink a glass of water and throw up and get it over with. Then I eat."

"I'll keep that in mind from now on."

"From now on, you'll be leaving at five a.m. for work. I doubt I'll be up until after you go." Although a good wife would get up and fix her husband a hearty breakfast before he went off to do the hard, physical work Win did. "I need a shower," she said.

"Me, too," he said, starting the water.

Together? she wondered. But no such luck. By the time she was done and dressed, he'd finished showering and had also gotten dressed. She decided not to let him get away with ignoring her.

"Last night you said you were tired, Win. What about this morning?"

"You were just sick."

"I'm fine now. In fact, I'm starved. But this time I'll fix breakfast for you."

"In a minute. First, I have something for you."

They went into the living room. On the coffee table sat a box wrapped in Christmas paper with a big red bow.

He remembered. Jenny's throat burned. For their wedding four years ago, when she'd given him the bolo tie he'd worn yesterday, she'd proclaimed it an early Christmas gift, turning an ordinary summer day into something special. He'd told her his family had ignored the holiday and probably would forever. How did you forget that your mother died on Christmas day?

He hadn't given her anything, hadn't even known it was traditional, but she hadn't cared at all. She'd just wanted him to have something from her and was pleased when he'd been so touched by it.

"I didn't get anything for you this time," she said, sitting on the sofa.

He sat next to her and laid a hand on her abdomen. "Yes, you did. But this is *your* early Christmas gift this time. It couldn't wait."

He set the box in her lap. She opened it carefully, intending to save the wrappings, then lifted the lid. Inside was a legal-looking document. She skimmed it then raised her eyes slowly to his.

"You got a loan for the lavender farm?"

"I have a job, a credit rating and savings."

She didn't know what to say, so she said nothing. He looked so proud and happy—

"The bank would only give us a loan on the property," he said, starting to look worried at her lack of reaction. "It wouldn't be enough to build any structures. I guess that's so they could recoup their losses, if necessary."

"Us?" she repeated, shaking her head. "This is *yours*."

"It's in both our names. We just have to make an offer on the property, get it accepted then sign the loan papers." He was waiting for her reaction.

"I appreciate what you did," she said.

He stiffened. "I hear a *but* in there."

She moved to the front window and looked out. "This is *my* dream, Win."

"Why can't your dreams be mine, too?"

"You'll want to provide input."

"What's wrong with that? Two heads are better than one, you know." He joined her at the window.

"Your father and Vaughn have said they would give us a second loan to get the initial structures up and running."

"What? You went to my *father?* My *brother?* And asked for *money?*"

"According to your business plan, it's going to take six months or more just to get the ground prepared and the plants in place in time for next year's growing season. We wouldn't borrow any money from your family until that's done. It'll be a long process, Jen. We'll do it in stages."

"We?"

"It's going to take both of us to get it off the ground. Trust me, it'll still be your project." He cupped her shoulder, but she jerked out of reach. "Why are you angry? You told me you couldn't qualify for a loan on your own. I could. You're my wife. What's mine is yours. What's wrong with that?"

Indeed. What was wrong with that? Because her pride had taken a beating? Did it matter? He was giving her the chance to fulfill her dream.

"I'm sorry," she said. "It just came as a shock."

"A happy shock, I hope."

He'd just wanted to please her. He'd done nothing but be supportive and caring and understanding. A lot of men wouldn't have reacted well to the situation that he seemed to take in stride.

She put her arms around him. "Thank you."

"You're welcome." He pressed his face into her shoulder and drew a deep breath. "I guess there'll be adjustments for both of us."

She didn't want to talk about it anymore, although they would need to at some point. Getting the loan for the land was one thing—that didn't change her plans. Borrowing from her father and brother was quite another.

"Time to eat," she said more brightly than she felt.

Just when they'd finished their pancakes and eggs, several trucks came up their driveway—her family, all except the new parents.

"What's going on?" Jenny asked her mother.

"We've come to gather the flowers and make bouquets for the farmers' market tomorrow," she said, setting her hand on Austin's shoulder. "We figure we'll be done in an hour or so, with this many people helping. At least, that's what Austin says. And since he and Annie have been doing this for two years, he's the expert. Okay, young man, lead the way."

Everyone listened to eleven-year-old Austin's instructions then got to work. Flowers were snipped, leaves stripped and bundles made— mixed bouquets and ones comprised of only one type of bloom, appealing to what Annie called a more sophisticated buyer. Pink and white asters, bright Shasta daisies, fragrant carnations and enormous red and yellow zinnias were plunked into the huge buckets of water and put in the barn until the next day. Tomorrow Jenny would pick the produce she planned to sell.

"How's baby Jamie?" Jenny asked her mother as they made and poured glasses of lemonade for everyone. Dori had brought a few dozen cookies, as well.

"Cute as a button. We stopped by the hospital on our way here."

"And Annie and Mitch?"

"On cloud nine. How about you?" The look she gave her daughter was searching and curious but not demanding. She wouldn't push Jenny for answers.

"I'm great. I'm sorry about the meltdown yesterday. Just an accumulation of stress that needed an outlet."

Dori nodded. "You got yourself a good man, honey."

"I know." *But he doesn't want me. He's just doing the right thing.*

"Then you know that all you need to do to make him happy is to love him. Everything else will fall into place." Dori held up a hand. "I've been observing. You're holding back from him. I'm not asking you why. I'm giving you the benefit of my years of experience. Don't hold back anything from him, good or bad. It'll come back to bite you."

Honesty. Win had made a point of it when they told their families about their situation. She should be as honest with him now. She should tell him she loved him, had loved him before, too, and all the years between.

Except…she really wanted to hear it from him first, as old-fashioned as that sounded. She'd worn her heart on her sleeve before. It was his turn now.

Patience. She needed to learn patience, something she wasn't always good at. He, on the other hand, was the very definition of it.

After her family left, she found Win in the barn. "Would you like to take a drive to see the property?" she asked. "Or maybe you already have."

"I trusted your research and plans. Yes, I would like that."

"I'll pack us a picnic."

Win watched her walk away. *Mine,* he thought. *All mine.*

Satisfaction settled over him, which was different from contentment, but it would do for now. The week between finding out she was pregnant and having the ceremony had been rushed and stressful for them both. For him, getting the loan arranged, dealing with his father—who'd barely spoken to him since—and spending every dinner being scrutinized by her family had worn him down, and he wasn't the one who was pregnant.

She came out of the house carrying a soft-sided thermal bag, the cardboard tube with the plans inside and a quilt, then they made the almost forty-five minute drive—much of it on an old, rock-studded dirt road—without saying much. Every so often he saw her eyes close for longer than a blink.

She came fully awake as they drove up the final stretch of road and reached the summit. Win rolled to a stop, turned off the engine and just sat there, staring.

"It's really something, isn't it?" she said, her gaze straight ahead, too.

He nodded, the view stealing his voice. The entire Red Valley stretched out in front of them, farms, fields and groves creating a perfect patchwork of color and texture. And smack in the center stood Gold Ridge Mountain, which even in late July was capped with snow. It towered, it glistened, it awed.

"Can you picture it?" Jenny asked, pointing. "The labyrinth over there. Row upon row of different varieties. Over there a gift shop, with an area where bridal parties can prepare. A distillery on the other side. Tucked back over among the trees, a B and B with a restaurant large enough to host receptions. Maybe even a spa. Think of the tourist draw. Imagine how beautiful it will be, and how incredible it will smell."

He'd turned to look at her as she spoke. "I can

see why you fell in love with it," Win said at the rapture in her expression.

They climbed out of the truck and carried the plans to a dilapidated picnic table, unrolling the pages, examining the details and discussing what should be done first and when. They examined the old plants, which hadn't been tended for years.

"They're hardy, in general," she said. "We can save money if we don't have to replace everything, but it's recommended they be replaced every five to ten years. It's probably been at least five years for these. The English variety has a better scent, but the French yields more oil."

"You know your family wants to help you clear the land and help with the planting, when the time comes. You need to let them, Jenny."

"But—"

"You would do the same for any of them. In fact, you would insist on it. Can you grow from seed rather than buy plants?"

"I was thinking I could install a high tunnel greenhouse or two here and start from seed, yes. Although maybe I should just ask Annie if I could put one up on her property. We'll probably be living there for a long time, anyway."

He looked around. "Would you like to build a house here?"

She shrugged. "Maybe something above the gift shop to live in during those few months where we'd be open to the public. I have to learn to be patient. It's going to take years to get everything done. And we'll have a child to consider."

Or two or three, he thought, anticipating the future, too.

"I'm hungry. Are you?" he asked.

They spread the quilt on the ground under a shady tree and ate sandwiches and potato salad, left over from their reception. He encouraged her to stretch out and close her eyes after they ate, her head in his lap. He ran his fingers through her hair, massaging her scalp long after she'd fallen asleep.

Win studied the land as unemotionally as possible. It was Jenny's dream, and he wanted to help her achieve it, but was it financially possible? He didn't know. What he did know was that it was going to take time, energy and heavy equipment to prep the land. And man-hours. Lots of man-hours.

He couldn't take on extra work for cash to help finance the venture and still have time to help out physically. She needed to let her family get involved.

After a half hour or so, she stirred, rolling onto her back and looking up at him, smiling. "Thanks. I needed that."

"It's been a good day. Tomorrow it's back to the salt mines for us."

"Are you sorry we didn't go to the hotel in Medford that Mom and Dad arranged for us?"

"I'm not much of a hotel guy myself."

"You just didn't want to say no to the gift." She sat up, sitting cross-legged, facing him.

He smiled slightly. Only an idiot would turn down a gift from his new in-laws. "It was thoughtful of them."

She laughed.

"Being here takes me back," he said, remembering that first summer, being outdoors every time they'd made love, although they'd never taken it slow and easy, or hesitated for any reason. They'd never known how much time and privacy they would have.

"We were lucky we never got caught. Really lucky," Jenny said. She took advantage of how easy things were between them to ask, "How much did it hurt that your father didn't come yesterday?"

"He said he wouldn't, so it wasn't a surprise."

She gave him a steady look. "That wasn't what I asked."

"I know. It stung, okay? But I don't have any expectations where he's concerned."

"Rose enjoyed herself, I think."

He nodded. "I'm glad she defied him. She needs to get out more. If you don't mind, maybe I'll bring her to the farm with me for dinner sometimes when I get off work."

"The more, the merrier." She yawned. "You'd think I hadn't already taken two naps today."

She wanted to ask why he was holding back. Desire had always been strong between them. They'd made a baby out of that desire—twice.

So what was stopping him now?

Ask him. The words shouted in her head this time. If she wanted an answer, she should just ask. But then she waited too long.

"Time to head home," he said.

And because she was afraid of his reasons, she agreed.

Later, when they got in bed, he seemed to expect it to be like the night before. He gave her a light kiss and rolled away from her. After a long, tense minute, she curled up behind him and put her arm around him. He covered her hand with his…

And went to sleep.

She would have it out with him, get to the bottom of his hesitation. They'd always been able to talk to each other. What was different now? It should be even easier. They were well and truly married with nothing to stop them from making love.

Tomorrow, she decided before she closed her eyes. Yes, tomorrow. She'd waited long enough.

Chapter Ten

Jenny startled awake when the alarm clock went off at 5:00 a.m. the next morning. Win hurried into the room.

"Sorry. I thought I'd turned it off."

"It's all right." She rose up on her elbows. He was dressed for work. "I should be a good wife and fix you breakfast, but I don't think I could stand the smell of anything."

"I'll eat with the hands at the ranch." He sat on the bed beside her and brushed her hair from her face, smiling. "The act of making breakfast doesn't make someone a good wife."

Now or never, she thought. He'd given her the

perfect opening. "I'd like to be the kind of good wife who makes love with her husband."

After a few seconds, he stood. "I gotta go."

"Why won't you talk to me about it, Win? You seemed relieved last night when I didn't push you for sex. Please, just tell me. Anything is better than my guessing. You were so adamant about being honest with my parents. Shouldn't you be honest with me, too?"

"Maybe tonight. Brody said he'd help you set up the booth at the market. I'll meet you there after work," he said tersely, not kissing her good-bye. "I'll call the Realtor about putting an offer on the property."

Jenny eyed the empty doorway. They'd had a good day yesterday, comfortable and relaxing. Now it looked like the honeymoon was over before it'd even begun.

She lay back and closed her eyes but couldn't go back to sleep. Finally she got up, drank a glass of water and dealt with her morning sickness. She took a quick shower, ate a bowl of cereal then went out to the garden to pick the produce for tonight's farmers' market.

Last year Annie had U-pick Saturdays open to the public for her berries then later in the year, pumpkins, but this year she'd found a buyer in San Francisco for all of that. She'd earned her organic status and with the help of a local restaurateur had found a strong market for her produce, especially her specialty lettuces and potatoes.

Maybe that's what she should be doing herself, Jenny thought, *instead of her grandiose plans.* Annie was smart. She'd specialized in a few products, lessening the chance for failure, whereas Jenny planned to enlarge her operation every year with a product that had a short selling period.

And now Win's cash and credit would be tied up with her dream, possible or not. She had to succeed, for his sake as well as her own.

What had she gotten herself—and her patient husband—into? She could easily end up ruining his finances.

Talk about pressure....

Jenny worked for a couple of hours then stopped to eat a handful of blueberries and a piece of toast with peanut butter. She'd just tugged on her work gloves when a white compact pickup pulled into her driveway. Her sister, Haley.

"Good morning," Haley said as she got out. She was the most serious of the Ryders. Ten years older than Jenny, they hadn't been particularly close but had been finding their familial connection over the past couple years when Jenny came home on break. She was taller than Jenny and thinner, but they shared the same auburn hair and Ryder blue eyes.

"It's my first full day off in weeks," her sister said as they hugged. "We've been down two physical therapists, but they finally hired one. She started at the rehab facility this morning, so I figured I'd see if you needed any help."

"I'm almost done. Want some lemonade? We can sit on the porch and talk."

"Sure, thanks." Haley followed Jenny into the house. "I stopped by the hospital. Mitch was picking up Annie and Jamie to take them home. Everyone is fine," she added before Jenny could ask. "That baby is so stinkin' cute."

"I'll go see them tomorrow. I have too much to do today."

"How are *you* doing?"

If Annie had been there, Jenny would've confided in her, but she was hesitant to be as open with her sister. Which made no sense. "I'm okay."

"No, you're not."

"Okay, no, I'm not, but I'm working on it." Tears pricked her eyes. "Sorry. Hormones."

"Apparently. After all, I've seen you fall off a horse and not shed a single tear, even though you broke your wrist."

"Because I was mad." Jenny plucked a tissue from a box on the counter and dabbed her eyes, the deluge over as fast as it had come.

"I remember." Haley accepted a glass of ice-cold lemonade. They went out to the porch. "I wanted to talk to you about Win's father."

"You know him?"

"I sat with Rose for a while on Saturday. Knowing I'm a PT, she mentioned that Shep seemed to be favoring his right leg, often limping by the end of the day, although he tries to hide it. Her imagination is going wild with possibilities, but he tells her it's nothing and refuses to see a doctor."

"If Rose can't convince him, I don't see how I can help."

"I wasn't thinking you so much as Win."

Jenny sort of laughed. "Honestly, I might stand a better chance than Win. Their relationship is rocky, to say the least. Why do you think Rose told you and not Win?"

"Shep ordered her not to, so she figured this was the way around it. She didn't specifically ask me to tell you and Win, but I know she expected me to." Haley leaned forward. "Someone needs to get through to him, Jen. Maybe it's deterioration that could be fixed with a knee or hip replacement. But maybe it's more than that. Maybe he fell from his horse and didn't tell anyone. The longer he puts it off, the less chance he has of a successful recovery and pain-free life."

"What is it about cattlemen?" Jenny asked. "Dad's the same way. If Mom weren't there to push him about his health, he'd be as stupidly stubborn about it as Shep."

"They pride themselves on their stoicism," Haley said.

"Men," Jenny said, summing it up, conveniently ignoring the fact that she had done the same thing when she'd broken her wrist.

They both laughed. "I imagine men say *women* in much the same way," Haley said.

"But we're perfect."

"Uh-huh. So, to change the subject completely, do you think you'll ever build a house on your ranch property?"

Vaughn and Mitch had built homes on theirs. None of the other siblings had yet, although they'd chosen their sites. "I don't know how Win would feel about that. We can't afford it right now, anyway, so we're lucky that Annie is happy having us live here. Why? Are you thinking about building on yours?"

"Maybe. The owners of the house I'm renting are putting it on the market. I'm tired of paying money to someone else, but I'm not sure I want to be that far out of town." She drew a circle on the wood planks with her toe. "I've been offered a job in Sacramento. I'd be heading up a team at a large rehab hospital. Lots of responsibility, and a huge increase in pay. Plus Sacramento's been named the best city for singles for several years. It's not too long a drive home, so I could be here for the big events."

Jenny sat back, a little stunned. "I guess I never thought about any of us leaving home. If it's what you want, of course you should do it. You can always come back."

Haley shoved herself off the glider, clearly agitated. "I haven't told you everything, and I *need* to tell someone everything. Will you keep it to yourself?"

"Of course I will." She joined her sister at the railing and rubbed her back. "What's going on?"

"I've also been offered a different job. Do you remember Clint Boone?"

"Vaguely. He went on the rodeo circuit after high school. He's still news in the Red Valley Press."

Haley nodded. "Did you see he broke his pelvis and other assorted bones in a competition last week?"

"I missed that."

"He'll be ready for rehab at home sometime in the next few weeks, and has asked me to be his private PT."

"Where?"

"On a spread he bought, maybe thirty miles from here."

Jenny couldn't get a handle on her sister's mood. Why was she so agitated? It seemed simple. She'd been made two offers. Choose one and be done with it. "Is it good pay?"

"He's mega rich, Jen, mostly from endorsements. He's very popular on the circuit. I quoted him a rate I thought he'd laugh it was so high, but he said okay, when could I start?"

Jenny smiled. "Called your bluff. That's interesting. I don't see your problem, unless… Do the two of you have a history?"

"One-sided, but yes."

"He pined for you?"

"No."

"Ah. And you don't think fourteen years of not seeing him is long enough to have killed that desire?"

"No."

Haley's tone was definite, which made Jen frown. "Why not?"

"I just know. If I see his picture in the paper or happen to catch him in an event being televised, that's all it takes."

"I'm not sure anyone *happens* to catch rodeo events on TV."

Haley glowered, which made Jenny laugh.

"It's not funny," Haley said. "I'd have my hands all over him. I don't think I could do that. And he's going to be surly because of his physical limitations and restless at not doing anything, and he'll try to rush his recovery, and we'd fight about it."

"Sounds terrible. And yet you're still considering it."

"He's my Achilles' heel, Jen. I worshipped him in high school. He didn't know I existed."

"Well, speaking from experience, I would tell you that you probably need to see it through, see what happens. But then, you'd be giving up a great job opportunity in Sacramento, one that may not come again for a long time. So, it comes down to your heart or your head. Which one wins?"

"I change my mind every five minutes."

"How soon do you have to decide?"

"By Friday for the Sacramento job. Clint won't be discharged from the rehab hospital for a while yet, but he's pushing for an answer."

"Is it possible to see Clint in person this week? Maybe you'll find there's really nothing there, so you wouldn't want to give up a lucrative job with a good, long-term future for a short-term job that might only cause you grief."

"He's in Kentucky."

"So? Planes fly there."

Haley went silent for a minute, then nodded. "That's exactly what I'll do. I'll make him pay for the ticket, too."

Jenny laughed. She'd never seen her sister so riled up. "Let me know if you need a ride to the airport."

"I will, thanks." She marched to her car, determination in every stride.

Still the serious one, Jenny thought, but with

a well of emotion she usually kept tamped down. It would be fun to watch her interact with Clint.

Jenny rinsed their lemonade glasses then decided to lie down for a few minutes. She'd just settled on the couch when the phone rang.

"I'm flying there on Thursday, but I'll drive myself to the airport. I'll only be gone overnight," Haley said. "I promised to find him someone else if I say no."

"I'm sure that made him happy."

There was a long pause. "I don't feel like myself, Jen."

"I know that feeling."

Jenny lay down again and closed her eyes but all she could see was the look on Win's face this morning when she'd told him, *I'd rather be a wife who makes love with her husband.*

She'd given her sister good advice, but now she needed to make a decision herself—heart or head. She only had about nine hours to make up her mind.

Win parked his truck near the farmers' market area, wondering if his wife would be speaking to him after he'd again avoided her question that morning. He hadn't even kissed her goodbye, which was juvenile behavior.

It had been on his mind all day.

What would it hurt to tell her the truth? There

were consequences to them making love, ones she seemed to be ignoring. Shouldn't they talk about it?

It was something his father would do—not try to explain. It turned Win's stomach that he might be like his father in any way.

In the middle of a transaction, Jenny smiled when she spotted him through the farmers' market crowd. He joined her in the booth but said nothing until she was free. She surprised him with a quick kiss and hug.

"It looks like you're almost sold out already," he said.

"Technically I am. What's here has been promised to others in the booths as trade. I'm getting honey and peaches in return. How was your day?"

"Fine. Are you hungry? I'm going to get a grilled sandwich. I can find something vegetarian for you."

"I'm good. Brenna James brought me a new dish to try from her restaurant."

"Okay. I'll be back."

Win enjoyed the routine of eating his dinner, listening to the music and watching Jenny behind the booth as she talked and laughed. He also enjoyed how she would glance his way now and then, as if making sure he was still there—and watching. As if that was important to her.

He hoped so.

People were warmer to him tonight, friendlier—or was it his imagination? By now everyone would've heard about their marital situation and the pregnancy, since nothing stayed quiet in Red Valley City for long. Undoubtedly the change in people's reaction to him spoke to Jenny's popularity—if she liked him, he must be okay.

Maybe he should've tried harder through the years to be a bigger part of the community. But mostly he'd done his job and little else. Fortunately he'd never caused any trouble, so he didn't have a reputation to live down.

At seven o'clock he and Jenny broke down the booth and headed home.

"Have you noticed your father limping lately?" she asked as they drove.

The out-of-the-blue question caught him off guard. "No. Why?"

"Rose confided in Haley, who confided in me so that I could confide in you, that your father's been having some trouble with his right leg, although Haley doesn't know whether it's his knee or his hip. Or something else altogether."

"Like what?"

"That's the question. You've never seen a hitch in his step? A grimace when he mounts or dismounts?"

"I rarely see him at all. When I do he's already on horseback, and so am I, and he's issuing orders."

"Maybe you should go out of your way to take a look for yourself. I mean, Rose must be sure something is wrong, since she's in the house with him and sees him walk."

"Has she talked to him about it?"

"Apparently she's pushed him toward seeing the doctor, but he refuses."

"What a surprise." He glanced at Jenny. "I can't imagine Rose thinking I'd have more luck convincing him. If she can't, who could?" *No one.* Win answered his own question.

Except…Win had to try. He couldn't know something was wrong with his father and do nothing, even though it would prompt yet another argument between them.

"Did you see the new baby today?" he asked, changing the subject.

"I took a nap during the only time I would've had free. I'll go tomorrow."

At the farm, they stowed everything. He'd stopped by to shower before meeting up with her.

"I'm going to clean up," she said, looking nervous suddenly.

"Okay." He didn't volunteer to join her, even though the thought of it had him creating scenarios in his head.

She emerged wearing the pink nightgown, and

determination in her eyes. Her hair was slicked back, her face shiny clean. She sat next to him on the couch, as close as she could get without actually touching him. Her hands shook as she shoved them through her wet hair, but when she spoke, her voice was strong and sure.

"I refuse to have a marriage of convenience."

Chapter Eleven

Anxious, Jenny waited for him to respond, getting more nervous by the second.

"I want to wait until your first trimester is over," Win said finally.

"Wait for what?"

"To make love."

She couldn't possibly have heard him correctly. "That's six weeks away."

"I know."

"Why?"

"Because it's sensible. And reasonable. Considering."

She was utterly confused. "Considering what?"

"The possibility of you having another miscarriage." He said it in a rush, as if he was ripping off the bandage, like they'd done with her parents.

Relief struck her first. "But you want me?"

His eyebrows drew together. "Of course I want you. Why would that change?"

"I was afraid..." She shook her head. She should've thought it through instead of reacting emotionally. She should've figured it out on her own. Could she have pregnancy brain, as Annie called it, this early?

"Do you remember what happened last time?" he asked, his gaze direct. "It was right after we'd had sex—a particularly enthusiastic experience, as you'll recall, because we'd been married for a few days and were enjoying the freedom that came with that. You even said so yourself—that it was different, being married. We both went a little wild."

"I remember."

"So we had that great night, then you miscarried right after. Right after. I don't want to take that chance."

"I wish you'd talked to me about this." Tenderness enveloped her. She reached for his hands. "I spoke with my doctor about it. She said just because it happened before didn't mean it would happen again. She emphasized it was as safe now as before, that it's unpredictable. If it's going to happen, it'll happen, whether or not we have sex."

He pulled his hands free. "When did you talk to her?"

"Last week."

"Why didn't you tell me?"

"I don't know. I just wanted to be sure of what we should and shouldn't do, so I asked." She hadn't wanted to grieve again, not if she could help it. According to the doctor she shouldn't do anything differently, not unless miscarriages became commonplace for her.

"You could have included me in the visit." He looked and sounded hurt—and was entitled to it all.

"You're right. I'm sorry." This whole being-a-couple thing was hard to get used to. She'd been independent for so long. Sharing everything wasn't coming naturally.

He's your husband. He gets to know this stuff.
I know. I know.

His expression slowly shut down to a blank indifference, then he looked away. "If you don't trust me enough to talk to me about these kinds of things, I don't know what we're doing here, Jen. I want to wait. Everything inside me says we should. You don't agree, I know, but for me the temptation to give in to my physical need is too great if I sleep next to you. I have to think about it. Maybe I should use the guest room for now."

He walked out of the house. When he hadn't returned after fifteen minutes, she decided to wait for him in their bedroom.

The double bed felt huge without him, and cold, even in the middle of summer.

And painfully lonely.

She didn't want him to be mad at her. Or even disappointed. And she didn't want to sleep alone, even without passion. Jenny ran her hand down his side of the bed. She dragged his pillow against her, buried her face in it. Maybe it was her imagination, but she could smell him in the fabric, making her eyes sting from the longing.

He's been good to you, beyond what you deserve for trapping him, no matter how unintentional. Show him it matters. That he matters. That you appreciate him.

She made her way through the house and stepped onto the porch. He didn't acknowledge her, just continued to stare at the night sky, the stars twinkling. A cool breeze carried the scent of carnations.

She went up behind him, wrapped her arms around his waist and rested her head against his back. "Come to bed, Win. I need you. Please. If we have to wait another six weeks for you to be comfortable, we'll wait. But I want you beside me."

Still he didn't turn around. "First question, Jen. Do you worry that if we lose this baby, I'll leave?"

She squeezed her eyes shut at the shocking directness of his question, and the fear that stabbed at her. "Yes."

"I didn't let you go for four years even though we never saw each other. I won't let you go this time, either."

Because you love me? Or because I'm legally yours, as you told my parents?

He finally faced her. "Second question. Your doctor really believes there's no danger?"

Hope did a pirouette on her heart. "No more or less than any other pregnancy."

She waited for him to respond. She swore she could hear a clock ticking somewhere, counting off their past, their present and their future, getting louder and louder as he looked at her in silence, not touching.

"Do people actually use the term *marriage of convenience* anymore?" he asked.

"I don't know. It fits, though." She was trying not to hold her breath as she waited for him to come to some sort of decision.

"Do you feel like we're strangers, Jen?"

"I don't understand the question."

"Technically we've been married for four years. We've slept together a lot. A whole lot. At least in the past. We're expecting a baby. But I never courted you, not in the traditional way. Did you miss that?"

"Sort of, but given our family histories we didn't have any choice." In truth, she'd mostly been happy sneaking off with him. "How about you?"

"Fantasies kept the relationship alive for me— remembering what really happened between us and imagining more. It's just…we never got to know each other well."

It wasn't until that moment that she also realized they hadn't. Not really. Even now they tiptoed around each other, testing each other's reactions. "I guess not."

He brushed her hair from her face then touched her ear, her cheek, her jaw. "I know that you like it when I kiss this spot under your ear." He leaned forward and did just that, sending shivers through her. "And I know you like it when I drag my tongue down your neck to between your breasts."

He brought his words to life. Jenny arched back, curving her arms around his head as he brushed his hand across her shoulder and down her arm, taking the skinny strap along.

"That's the sort of thing I know about you," he said. "How you react when I do that. How I react."

Was he going to tease her or take it all the way? Had he come to accept that there was no danger in consummating their marriage, after all? Six weeks was a very long time to wait, especially sharing a bed every night.

"How does a man court his own wife?" he asked. But was there really an answer?

"I'd say you wrote the book on it," she said, finding it hard to breathe when he dragged his fingertips over her body.

"This is foreplay, not courtship."

"At the moment, I don't need either one."

Win leaned back and looked into her eyes, judging for himself. Then he gently, carefully kissed her. That was all it took. He wasn't the one to ramp things up. She was. She wanted him fiercely, completely. She lunged at him, clung to him, demanded of him. He tried to slow things down. She wasn't allowing it.

He kissed her, long and hard, drawing flattering sounds of need. The freedom of being married to her notched up the pleasure to an unrivaled level. He laid a hand gently on her breast. "Too tender?" he asked.

She shook her head, pressing his hand more firmly against her. He nestled his face between her breasts, listened to her heart thump against her chest, and got a little nervous that she was too excited.

"Please, Win. You can drag it out the next time. Right now I just need you."

It was a command he felt a need to obey, for

both of them, so he lifted her into his arms and carried her inside. Her nightgown slipped down and off before she got into bed, holding her arms out to him. He pulled off his clothes, tried to slow his need, but she was every dream, every fantasy come true.

"Don't wait," she said, pleading. "Just come inside me. Now. Please, Win. Now."

He joined with her in a melding that was fast and intense and gratifying beyond belief, his hot skin moving against hers, her legs wrapped around him. He cupped her rear, bringing her higher, closer. He gave, she took. He took, she gave. They kissed, long, openmouthed, wet kisses as sounds of need rose from them. The hunger built, needing satisfaction. Finally, mutually, it happened in an endless, soaring moment of completion, like nothing they'd ever experienced.

Then before he collapsed on her, he rolled, taking her along, nestling her on top of him, her legs between his.

"Next time we'll go slow," she said, her breath shaky against his neck, her body damp and warm.

"We can give that a shot, I suppose."

He felt her smile against his skin.

"You may get tired of me and my demands, husband."

"Doubtful, wife." He stroked her back. "You're feeling all right?"

"It's safe to say I feel better than I have in my entire life."

"Me, too." And that was the truth. Nothing else even came close. Not even their affair four years ago, which was only about sex. This was…so much better.

"First time in a bed," she said.

"I'm sure that's what made it particularly good."

She laughed. Then they rolled to their sides. He circled her nipples with his finger. "There are changes here already. Will you breast-feed?"

"Definitely."

"Good."

"The timing could've been better," she said. "March due date. I should be planting the seeds about then."

"Will you try to build the gift shop for next summer's opening?"

"I won't have product to distill yet. I'm even debating opening to the public next year."

"You wouldn't have any income to make the loan payments."

"I would if I grow for someone else next year and sell the whole crop." She pressed a kiss to his throat. "Enough business."

"Even funny business?" It was the most relaxed they'd been with each other since she'd come back to the Red Valley. He didn't want it to end, but he had the feeling that as the realities of getting a business off the ground became clearer, it would affect their relationship, too, in ways they probably couldn't even anticipate at the moment.

"I need to get up for a minute first." She planted a kiss on his lips, then rolled out of bed.

He enjoyed watching her walk out of the room and looked forward to watching her walk back.

"Win!"

He flew out of bed at the panic in her voice.

"There's...there's blood. There's blood."

His heart slammed into his chest, but he forced himself to stay calm, for Jenny's sake. "I'll get the phone. Don't move."

He was gone for less than ten seconds. He punched the speed dial for her obstetrician that he'd added just yesterday. Her answering service picked up.

"This is Win Morgan. I need to speak to Dr. Saxon right away." He was put on hold.

Jenny's face was ashen, her breathing shallow. "I can't lose this baby," she whispered. "I can't. Please."

"What's going on, Win?" Dr. Saxon asked. He appreciated her directness.

"Jenny and I just had sex for the first time. She's bleeding."

"How much?"

"A little. Spotting."

"Cramps?"

"Do you have cramps?" he asked his wife.

"No."

"I heard her," the doctor said. "It's not uncommon, Win, and it doesn't mean she's miscarrying. I want you to monitor her closely through the night. If the bleeding continues, especially if it gets heavier or she starts to cramp, take her to the hospital right away. They'll call me. Okay?"

Fear the likes of which he'd never known lassoed him and yanked tight. "Okay."

"Stay calm. Help Jenny stay calm. Chances are it's nothing of consequence. Tomorrow morning, first thing, bring her in."

He hung up then repeated what the doctor said. Jenny laid her head on his shoulder as he crouched in front of her. He was calling himself all kinds of names in his head. He knew he should've left her alone. Knew it. He would never let her sway him from his resolve again.

But he said, "Let's get you to bed, Jen."

"I need to clean up first. Not a bath. Just a quick shower."

They got in the tub together. He washed her gently. Her eyes looked huge, her face gaunt, even her body seemed to shrink.

"Do you want me to call your mom?" he asked as she got into bed. "Or someone else?"

"I want you. Just you."

Relief washed over him. That was progress,

in his mind. "Would you like a glass of water? Iced tea?"

"Water, please."

He started to leave, but she grabbed his arm. "Fifteen seconds, Jen," he said.

He was true to his word. As she drank he finger combed her hair. "You need to relax. I know it's hard, but it's better for you and the baby."

"I won't be able to sleep."

"I'll stay awake for both of us. You rest. I promise I'll wake you every hour so that you can see for yourself."

He got her settled, although she dug her fingers into his arms for a long time before she finally loosened her grip and gave in to sleep. He would have to call his father early in the morning.

Throughout the night they checked, finding only a small bit of spotting the first time. After that, nothing. Then in the morning, they were already at the doctor's office when Dr. Saxon arrived. The fiftyish woman had a single practice and delivered all her babies, no other doctors on call for her. She probably had never had a vacation because of that choice.

"You beat my staff," the doctor said, "but come on back. We'll do the paperwork after. How'd it go during the night?"

Jenny came out of her stupor. "It stopped."

"Good. Undress from the waist down." She gave

Jenny a sheet. "You know the drill. You staying?" she asked Win.

"Yes."

Jenny heard the steel in his voice. He'd been calm and quiet all night. In control. But she could see a break in that control now that someone else was in charge.

Dr. Saxon didn't leave the room, but got out the supplies she needed and started the exam immediately.

"So it was the first time you had intercourse since you got pregnant, Jenny?" she asked.

"Yes."

"And maybe you both were a little enthusiastic?"

Win made a slight sound at the question. Jenny eyed the doctor from her position between her upraised knees. "He was trying to be gentle. I was the one who was overly enthusiastic."

"She told me you said it was fine to have sex," Win said, his voice harsh, accusatory.

"I stand by that, Win. There was no reason not to." She rolled her chair back a foot. "Well, it looks like you've got a small tear, but that's all. That's where the blood came from. The uterus and everything else is fine."

Win took her hand. Jenny squeezed it hard.

"I would suggest you hold off for a few days, then proceed with a little more caution," Dr. Saxon said, a twinkle in her eyes. "Be creative in the meantime. It'll be good for both of you to enjoy yourselves."

"It's all right for her to stay by herself today?" Win asked.

"Perfectly." She cocked her head, listening. "Marnie just arrived. She'll take care of the forms. You have your next appointment?"

"In three weeks."

"Good. I'll see you then." She looked at Win. "You did the right thing by calling me last night. I'm glad it was a false alarm. There's no reason to feel guilty, so wipe that from your mind."

They climbed into his truck a few minutes later. "I should get to work," he said.

Jenny knew he was reluctant to leave her alone. "I don't have much to do today at the farm. Nothing that couldn't wait until tomorrow. Why don't you just drop me at the homestead. I'll spend the day with Mom, go see Annie and the baby. You can pick me up when you're done."

"That's good." He started the engine. "I like that plan."

"I thought you might." She reached across the seat for his hand. "I'm sorry for the scare last night. Guess I'm going to have to tone down my enthusiasm." She grinned at him, hoping he would smile back. Sex had always been the biggest part of their relationship. If they didn't have that…

"You just need to let me be the boss," he said.

"Is that right? I don't remember the word *obey* in our vows. In fact, I distinctly remember having the man who married us take it out."

"You made quite a fuss about it, as I recall."

"It was important." She couldn't tell for sure if he was teasing her.

He gave her a quick glance. "Will you tell your mom what happened last night?"

"No."

"She's going to wonder why you're spending the day. She'll see it in your eyes that something happened."

"Well, then, maybe you should just take me to the farm instead." She crossed her arms. She didn't like it when he was...

Right.

He took the road to the homestead, not the farm.

"My family doesn't need to know everything, Win. Being honest about our marriage and the pregnancy was one thing, but overenthusiastic sex is entirely different."

He finally grinned. "You're right."

"It was really good though," she said.

"It was. And I'm looking forward to following the doctor's orders and being creative with you. I wouldn't mind if you'd wear that pink number again."

"Okay." Her pulse jumped and bounded at the

mere thought. There was so much about him to discover and enjoy—and delight in.

He studied her for a moment. "That's bettter. Now you can face your mom without her asking what's wrong. All she'll see is a satisfied bride."

"Bragger."

He lifted her hand to his lips for a moment, and she melted. She'd never expected him to be romantic, but she was sure glad he was. Was he intent now on courting her?

She wouldn't complain about that. Whatever the reason for their marriage—whether it was for the baby's sake or saving face with their friends and family—they were entitled to find happiness within the relationship.

Courtship, even if after the fact, was a good start. And it didn't have to be one-sided, either. Whether or not he would agree, he'd been courting her. What did he call the gift of securing the loan, if not courtship?

She just had to be as clever in return.

Chapter Twelve

From a distance Win watched his father dismount and lead his horse into the stable. Rose was right. He was limping.

Win nudged his horse. Usually he avoided being in the stable at the same time as his father. This time he planned it. He wasn't looking forward to the discussion.

His father looked up, startled when Win dismounted outside the doorway and led his horse inside. Shep had begun toweling down his horse. He couldn't just walk away.

"We'll start moving the herd tomorrow," Win said.

"If you can manage to be on time."

"I told you why I was late, Dad. Jenny had a doctor's appointment."

"Women have been havin' babies since the dawn of time. If it's s'posed to be, no doctor's gonna make a difference."

Win counted to ten. "Husbands tend to be a little more involved with their wives' pregnancies these days."

"You gonna be takin' a lot of time off for doctor visits and such?"

"It's unpredictable. Why? You thinkin' about replacing me?"

"If I need to."

"I pull my own weight. And I make up for time lost." Win started grooming his horse, a task that generally soothed him. "I noticed you were limping."

"When?"

"When you led Zeke into the barn."

"Just a little hitch after a day in the saddle. It's already worked itself out."

It was unusual for his father to carry on a conversation, which probably was a good indication he was lying—to himself and to Win, trying to talk them both out of thinking anything was wrong.

Win didn't want to involve Rose, so he said, "I've noticed it before. It's gotten worse."

"Mind your own business."

"You are my business, like it or not."

His father glared at him.

"Did you take a fall?"

He snorted. "Not hardly." He started brushing his horse's mane.

"Is it your hip or your knee?" They worked side by side, not looking at each other.

"You act like I'm an old man. I'm sixty, not decrepit."

"Plenty of sixty-year-olds have hip and knee replacements."

"They don't have ranches to run."

Ah. So he did know he had a problem. "You think I can't run this place while you recuperate? Carlos has been your foreman for thirty years. I've been working since I was eight. I think we can manage."

"You're not even livin' here anymore. Wouldn't surprise me if you end up working at the Ryder place, you with your newfangled ideas."

The fury in his father's voice struck hard and deep in Win, who moved closer to him and kept his voice low. "Like it or not, I'm your son. What happens to this ranch matters to me. But if you want to drive me away, you keep on talking, old man."

Win stalked away. He caught up with one of the hands and asked him to finish grooming his horse, then he got in his truck and headed for home—to his wife, another sometimes stubborn person, but one who at least had faith in him.

On the drive, he called his sister. "I talked to him," he said. "He sort of admitted to having a problem, but that's as far as I could get with him. Maybe you could talk to Doc Wheeler, see if he'd come to the ranch."

"He'll think we're ganging up on him," Rose said.

"We are."

She laughed a little. "Okay. I'll try."

A few minutes later, Win parked in front of the Ryder homestead. Jenny and her mother were sitting in rocking chairs on the porch, sipping something cold. Jenny not only smiled at him, but got up to greet him as he climbed the steps, giving him a kiss and hug. He wanted to relax into her, to hold her for a while, to feel welcome, unlike at his own family's ranch.

Jim came out from the house with two beers and passed one to Win. A few minutes later Adam and Brody joined them, then Vaughn, Karyn and Cassidy came in their truck.

"Are you having a party?" He'd almost said *another* party. It was a more-than-once-a-week event for them.

"Just dinner," Dori said. "If you and Jen would like to stay, there's plenty."

He looked at his wife, who shrugged, as if to say it was his decision, which left him stuck. He wouldn't mind having dinner with them, to let their uncomplicated family life dispatch his conversation with—and worries about—his father.

"Do I have time to go home and shower?" he asked. Which would serve two purposes. He would wash the ranch off him and it would give him a little breathing space to recover from the bitter conversation with his father.

"Is an hour enough?" Dori asked.

"Plenty. Thanks."

"Maybe you should leave a change of clothes here for future occasions."

He nodded, then he looked at Jenny. "I'll be back soon."

"I'll go with you," she said. "Let me grab my purse."

He didn't know why that made him happy, but it did. It lifted the weight off him in a big way.

His father-in-law dropped a hand on Win's shoulder and steered him away from the porch, out of hearing range.

"My daughter seems happier than she's ever been," Jim said. "I just want to thank you for that. I'm proud to call you son."

Win's throat closed. Why couldn't his own father tell him he was proud of him? "Thank you, sir. That means a lot."

Jenny came down the steps, watching them, curiosity in her eyes. She held out a hand to her husband. He took it. She didn't argue about him opening the truck door for her, nor when he offered to help her climb in. Maybe he would hear about it in a minute, when they were on the road. She valued her independence and competence a lot.

But she just settled back and smiled, as if intentionally baffling him was her goal. "I got to hold the baby today. Haley called him stinkin' cute. I have to agree."

"How's Annie?"

"Back to her calm self. I asked her for labor and delivery details but she refused to share. She said we could watch the scary birthing videos in the classes, like everyone else."

Win laughed. It felt good, having a normal conversation. "I called the Realtor and gave her the price we want to offer on the land. We need to go to her office tomorrow and sign some paperwork."

"Okay. Do you want to do it at your lunch break or at the end of the workday?"

"We're starting to move the herd to the next pasture tomorrow. We'll eat on the run."

"You can just call me when you're done for the day and I'll meet you."

Yeah, everyday conversation between a husband and wife. He'd feared they would never reach that point.

They entered the house through the side entrance, directly into the laundry area. He shook off his dusty clothes outside then draped them over the washer, intending to wear them the next day.

She had the shower turned on and the water at a perfect temperature when he went into the bathroom. Her eyes sparkled, her lips curved in a knowing smile. But knowing what?

"Something you want to say, Jen?" He stripped off his briefs and dropped them on the floor. Her expression alone excited him.

She moved close and wrapped her hand around him. "Take your shower. I've got a surprise for you."

Then she left. Just like that.

He couldn't remember taking a quicker shower. He toweled off, wrapped it around his hips and went in search of her. He didn't have far to go. She'd pulled back the bedding and was stretched out on the bed, wearing only a bra and panties.

She patted the spot next to her then crooked her finger at him.

His hesitation felt like an hour. "The doctor said—"

"We should get creative. That's what I'm doing. Lie down, husband."

"We'll be late for dinner."

"We're newlyweds. They'll wink at each other and expect us to smile with satisfaction."

"You have all the answers."

"I even know the questions."

He stretched out beside her. "Like what?"

"Like would my husband like me to tease him for a long time or just get right to it?"

He sucked in a quick, hard breath as she put her mouth on him. "And the answer?" he managed to ask.

"This *is* the answer."

Getting right to it. And man, was she ever. Her mouth was warm and wet as she aroused, tempted and teased. Her fingers found places to explore, taking him beyond earth, letting him free fall awhile, then picking up the slack again, until he couldn't hold back and she didn't try to make him. She honored him, celebrated him in a way she never had before.

And he gloried in it.

Spent, he pulled her close, felt her breath against his neck, warm and unsteady. He toyed with the catch on her bra.

"Nope," she murmured. "This one was just for you. You can take a turn in a couple of days, if you want." She stretched leisurely, giving him an eyeful as her newly enlarged breasts mounded above her bra.

After a few minutes of just lying there together, he said, "We should probably get dressed and go."

"If we must." She sat up and smiled at him. "But here's something to think about. I have plans for you for later. This time the answer to the question will be that my husband would like me to tease him for a long time."

She got out of bed, a self-satisfied smile on her face, fully aware that he would be thinking only about that all through dinner with her family. With her father looking him in the eyes and calling him son.

Oh, yeah. Win was enjoying this marriage business a whole lot.

"You understand there are six heirs," Realtor Ellen Travis said to Win and Jenny late the next afternoon as they signed the offer documents. "Not only will it take a little time to get in touch with everyone, reaching accord with that many people can be very difficult. Some won't accept less than the listing price. Some will be happy just to be done with it."

"I think we offered a fair price," Jenny said. "I did a lot of research on it."

"I know you did. I'm just letting you know that it may take weeks before we have a final answer."

"I'm prepared for that." She looked at Win, who had let her take charge, since she'd done all the prep. "We know we won't be able to get started until next spring, so if it drags on until then, that's okay. No payments to make in the meantime."

"Well, you don't want it to drag on for too long. Right now you've got the loan lined up. If your financial situation changes in any way before the offer is accepted, you could lose the loan." Ellen held up a hand. "Just saying."

Which worried Win a little. Doc Wheeler had showed up before office hours, at Rose's request, and they'd gotten into a row, with his father chasing off the doctor and telling him never to come back.

After that, his father refused to speak to Win, except to tell him to stay out of his life, then gave him orders through the foreman all day—unnecessary orders, since Win had been moving herd since he was a boy.

Rose had been humiliated by the scene with the doctor, and Win wondered if he would be fired, a threat he would now be living with as long as he worked for his father. If Win was let go, it would change their financial situation in a drastic way. They would lose the chance to own the property—and therefore Jenny's dream. He would end up letting her down before their marriage got off the ground.

They were both quiet as they left the Realtor's office, letting it all sink in.

"Nothing is easy, is it?" she said finally.

He shook his head. "How about dinner and a movie, wife?" he asked. "Take our minds off it all." They'd never been on a date before, he realized, which seemed funny, considering everything.

"I think that sounds great."

But as they got into his truck, his phone rang. "Hey, Rose. What's up?"

"I just called 911. Dad fell. I think he broke his leg."

Chapter Thirteen

"That was about as bad a break as I've seen. You shattered your femur," the all-business orthopedic surgeon said to Shep as Win, Jenny and Rose stood by in the hospital room. "And you need a hip replacement. We'll do it all at once. How long have you been in pain?"

Shep stared out the window, not answering.

"You have severe arthritis in your right hip, Mr. Morgan," the doctor continued. "And your left hip will be a candidate for replacement within a few years, as well. Plus you have osteoporosis, which is why you were susceptible to this severe of a break at your age."

Still nothing. Jenny could feel Win's frustration at his father's silence. Rose wrung her hands.

"When will the surgery be performed, Doc-tor?" Jenny asked.

"Tomorrow morning." He moved closer to his patient. "We'll have you up on your feet with a walker almost right away. You can probably go home on the third or fourth day, provided you have everything set up to care for you, including a phys-ical therapist, whether you go to the rehab center or they come to you at your home. Barring that, you could be an inpatient at a rehab facility instead."

"My sister is a PT," Jenny said. "She won't be available, but I'm sure she can help us find some-one to come to the ranch. Do you want me to ar-range that, Mr. Morgan?"

His silence continued.

The doctor met Jenny's glance for a moment. "The patients who recover the fastest, Mr. Mor-gan, are the ones who do the therapy faithfully and thoroughly, and you strike me as a man who wants a quick recovery. On the other hand, if you try to do too much too soon, you can undo prog-ress in a hurry. Probably for the first time in your life, you're going to have to follow orders instead of give them."

Shep's frown deepened.

"Your short-term recovery should be four to six weeks. Long term is anyone's guess. It depends on your involvement and desire to heal. So, any questions? No? Then I'll see you in the morning."

"Are you in pain now, Dad?" Rose asked, fussing with his pillows.

"No."

"Would you admit it?" Win asked. "This isn't the time for heroics. Keeping you out of pain helps with healing and recovery."

"Leave me alone. All of you." He closed his eyes.

"I'll be taking over at the ranch, Dad," Win said. "Anything in particular you want to tell me?"

He didn't bother to open his eyes. "You wanted a chance to prove yourself. Apparently you got it."

Win, Jenny and Rose walked out of the room and down the hall to the waiting room, where there was no chance Shep might overhear them.

"I need to get to the ranch," Win said. "Probably have to hire another hand to help out for a while. Are you staying here, Rose?"

"For now, but I'll need to figure out what to do about meals for the hands tomorrow. Maybe Carlos's wife would pitch in."

"Do you want to call her or should I?"

"You can, if you don't mind."

"How about you, Jen?" Win asked. "Stay or go?"

Jenny hesitated. She felt like she should keep

Rose company, especially since Shep didn't want anyone with him.

"I'm not hanging around more than an hour," Rose said before Jenny could answer. "I'll be fine."

"I'll be here with you all day tomorrow," Jenny told her.

"Call if you need anything," Win said to his sister, giving her a hug. "He's tough. He'll be fine."

"Will he ride again?" Her eyes were wet with tears.

"I don't know."

"He wouldn't want to live, Win."

He nodded, then he took Jenny's hand, holding tight as they walked away. "I never thought I'd see my father helpless."

"Do you think he'll follow the doctor's orders?"

"Your guess is as good as mine. I don't envy the PT who ends up working with him."

They climbed into the truck and headed out. "You can leave me at the homestead," she said. "That way if you end up working so late you need to stay overnight, you know I'll be fine."

"Thanks." He glanced at her. "This isn't the way I wanted him to involve me more."

"He'll be home issuing orders in a few days, so you really won't have a chance to make any changes," she said. "He'll be burning up your walkie-talkies all day long."

Win smiled. "Yeah, you're right about that." He put a hand on her thigh. "How're you doing?"

Earlier she'd readied a huge order that'd been picked up that afternoon for the San Francisco market, then they'd met the Realtor, then Shep… "It's been a long day, but at least I get to be fawned over by my mother. You've got the tough job."

"I'm up to it."

"I have no doubt about that, Win. Do you and the foreman get along? Will there be a power struggle with him?"

"Good question. Guess I'll find out. Regardless, as you pointed out, Dad will be home and on his dictator's throne soon."

They turned onto the road leading to Ryder Ranch, then the long driveway. As soon as they pulled up, her mother and father came out to the porch, Adam and Brody behind them.

Win filled them all in. Her mother packed dinner for him to take. As she handed him the plastic container, Adam said, "You know, Win, I could come help you finish moving the herd tomorrow. We're not moving ours until next week."

"Me, too," Brody said.

Win looked startled, then a little overwhelmed. Jenny slipped her hand into his.

"I appreciate the offer. I do. But if my father knew…"

"Why would he?" Brody said. "He won't be

there. We'll be gone before he gets out of surgery, probably. It's what family does, Win. You'd do the same for us."

"Thanks. Can I let you know later? I need to talk to the foreman first."

"I can go over and fix the meals for your hands," her mother said. "I'd just need to talk to Rose and get a plan figured out."

He swallowed hard and nodded, touching the brim of his hat.

Jenny walked him to the truck. The fact he couldn't say anything told her all she needed to know. He simply kissed her goodbye and left.

She thanked every one of her family with hugs. "I need to call Haley."

Her mother pointed as her sister's car came up the driveway. "She said she had something to talk to us about. I'm not sure how many more surprises we can take this month." Dori winked. "I'd love to hear she's met *the one.*"

Give it a day or two, Jenny thought, *and you might.*

The Ryder family shared a meal of enchiladas, chile rellenos, beans and rice. Haley told them about the two job offers.

"Sacramento," Dori said, her voice hushed.

"Sweetheart," Jim said. "It's her life. Her decision. She wouldn't be moving to Maine, after all."

"I think I can fly to Maine faster than I can drive to Sacramento."

"Mom, really," Haley said. "I promise I won't miss an important occasion. We can meet halfway for lunch sometimes."

"Well, I vote for this Clint Boone person."

"Careful what you wish for, Mom," Adam said. "I remember Clint from high school. I'm not sure you'd want one of your baby girls to live with the guy."

"Live with? You didn't say anything about that, Haley."

"He wants live-in help. If I decide to do it, I'll take a leave of absence from my job, not quit. It would only be for a couple of months."

The conversation shifted to another topic. It wasn't until after dinner that Haley and Jenny were able to catch a few minutes alone. They sat on a glider in the garden.

"Correct me if I'm wrong," Jenny said. "But reading between the lines of what you said, it sounds to me like you've made up your mind about which job. That job being Clint."

"I hadn't until tonight. Being here with everyone, even with part of our group missing? I would miss you all too much." She shrugged. "I won't decide until I see him, of course, but I figure other jobs like the Sacramento one will come up again."

"I'm sure you're right," Jenny said.

"Now, as to a PT for your father-in-law. Since he wouldn't want a Ryder as his PT, I've got someone in mind. She retired last year, but if we can talk her into it, she'd be perfect. She wouldn't let Shep run roughshod over her for a second."

"Someone I would know?"

"Frannie Upton. She moved here while you were away at college. Should I call her?"

"Please."

Haley nodded. "Is Win shell-shocked?"

"Yes. Not surprisingly."

"My guess is that he's most stunned at the support he's getting here. I don't know him very well yet, and I've only seen him a few times, but it's obvious he loves you."

Obvious? Really? Jenny didn't see it. Yes, he took good care of her. Yes, he was kind and considerate. They were bound to each other. But love? Wouldn't he have said so by now?

You haven't told him, either.

No, she hadn't. Decisions had been made *for* them lately, choices made without options for either of them because they'd needed to do what was right. At least she wanted to hear him say the words first. He'd had that privilege from her years ago. It was her turn.

"He's a good man," Jenny said just as Win phoned her. "How's it going?"

"Not bad. Carlos and I are figuring things out.

His wife is willing to do the cooking when Rose can't, so please tell your mom thanks for the offer. If Adam and Brody want to help move the herd, I'd be grateful. With Dad gone and me at the hospital tomorrow, we're short two."

"I'll tell them. Are you staying there tonight?"

"Do you mind? I want to go over the books while I've got the chance, see where he stands. Good thing he hasn't figured out the computer yet, so I won't need a password."

With a wave and smile, Haley went into the house, leaving Jenny alone. "I keep thinking about last night," she said into the phone.

"Me, too." His tone of voice was everything she wanted it to be—sexy, full of promise of another night of pleasure. "Bed's gonna be lonely tonight."

"I've kind of gotten used to you being next to me," she said. *Tell me you love me, then I know everything will be okay.*

"It wasn't much of an adjustment for me, either. Except for the way you take up most of the bed."

She smiled at the exaggeration. "I'm two people in one package."

"Why do I have a feeling you're gonna use that excuse for just about everything for the next seven months?"

"Because you know me that well."

Silence fell between them. She held her breath,

waiting, but all he said was, "Call me when you're going to bed to say good-night."

"Sure." She almost hung up but Haley came out the back door and held up a hand.

"Tell Win that Frannie begrudgingly said okay, as a favor to me. One item ticked off your list."

When Jenny hung up a couple of minutes later, it was with a light heart. She liked that her husband had come to depend on her some, that he turned to her during a crisis, that he allowed her family—now his family, too—to help. A lot of men wouldn't do that.

Maybe he had something to prove to his father and knew he didn't have time to do it alone. Actually, that was probably the most likely reason.

But it also proved what a smart man she'd married.

She could live with that.

"Everything went well," the surgeon said the next morning after a long time in the operating room. "He'll be out of recovery and back in his room in a couple of hours. Go get something to eat. Relax. He's going to be cranky when he wakes up. I've ordered his pain meds on the pump, that way he doesn't have to let anyone know when he's hurting. I figured out yesterday that he needs to be in control."

Rose laughed shakily. Jenny hugged her.

Win stood paralyzed for a few seconds. He loved his father. He'd thought that emotion had died years ago, but it had only gone into protective custody. Whether his father lived or died mattered to Win.

He held out a hand to the surgeon before he left, and said thank you.

And meant it even more than he'd expected.

A couple of hours later, they went into the hospital room. His father's eyes were closed. He looked frail, a word Win never would've applied to Shep Morgan. Win and Rose hung back, but Jenny, whom Win was coming to admire more than anyone on earth, went right up to her father-in-law and kissed his cheek.

"Welcome back, Dad Morgan," she said.

His eyes fluttered open. His usually clean-shaven face was dusted with gray stubble. He looked hard at Jenny, who smiled back.

"We're all here," she said. "Your son and daughter. And me. And your grandchild-to-be." She rested a hand on her abdomen and smiled at Win, who felt like he'd been punched in the gut, the emotional impact was so enormous.

Rose came forward and kissed her father's cheek as well.

Then Win forced himself to his bedside. "Everything's good at the ranch," he said, figuring his father would want that information first, although one of the first discussions they would have would be about the finances. Win had been shocked by the numbers.

His father didn't say anything, but he held Win's gaze for a long time, as if trying to figure out who he was, then his eyes closed and he went to sleep without a word of acknowledgment.

Some things never changed. Maybe Win should take comfort in that.

Chapter Fourteen

"That's it, Mr. Morgan. I quit."

Win stopped just inside the front door and listened to what had become an almost daily threat from the physical therapist, Frannie Upton, since she'd started coming eleven days ago.

"Fine by me, woman."

"I told you not to call me that. I am Ms. Upton."

"You are Ms. Uppity."

Win laughed. A moment later he encountered Rose with her hand over her mouth, too, her eyes twinkling.

Ms. Upton rushed out of the den/therapy room

and past Win and Rose, her tote bag in hand, muttering, "He's impossible. I won't be back."

"See you tomorrow," Win said as the front door slammed shut. She was a small, wiry woman with steely eyes and a just-as-steely constitution. It probably wasn't the best time to have a talk with his father, but Win had put it off long enough.

The ranch had been running smoothly without his father's help, a fact that angered and annoyed the man. Win was going to give him something else to irritate him.

He moved quietly into the den and caught his father with his head down, looking exhausted. One of the fights he and Ms. Upton always had was about him working too hard when she wasn't there, which was probably why she'd quit again.

"Dad?"

His head came up. "What *now?*"

Win pulled up a chair. "I'll be leaving a couple hours early tonight, but since I came in an hour early and worked through lunch, I figure it's even."

"I don't know why you bother to tell me. You do what you want, anyway."

"If I did what I want, I'd be changing this operation to one like the Ryder's. Organic/humane is the way to go, Dad."

"You know how much it costs to do that? And how long it takes? We'd have to build a closed herd.

We wouldn't make money for at least a couple of years, probably, and then only a small amount."

Win was prepared for the argument. "About that. I had a look at the books while you were in the hospital. All these years you've been griping about money, and you've got more than you need to run this place for twenty years. What's with that, Dad? You've been paying minimum wages to the hands. Hardly more'n that to me. I find that criminal. Inexcusable."

Shep tossed his head. "That's sound business. I've got money saved up for rainy days. Most people in this business can't afford to do that. I run in the black. I'm proud of that."

Win pulled a folded piece of paper from his pocket and passed it to his father. "That's what you owe me in decent back wages. You could see fit to give bonuses to the men who've been here for years, too."

Shep looked at the sheet and laughed. "In your dreams, son. You don't like the pay, quit. You sure as hell aren't gettin' back wages when you go." He leaned forward. "Don't think I don't know what's goin' on with you. You need a job or you can't buy that useless piece of property old lady Carson owned. Maybe Jimbo Ryder will give you a job so his princess doesn't starve, but adding you on would mean driving his profits too low, and he'd be one angry man, 'specially if you start demanding bigger wages than his sons."

Why had he ever thought anything would be different? Win wondered. Why? Shep Morgan would die the bitter man he was. A rich, bitter man.

But he was also right about one thing. Win couldn't quit. Without his job there could be no bank loan, therefore no lavender farm, therefore no happy wife.

He wanted a happy wife.

He passed a notebook to his father. "Here's an overview of what it would cost to convert the ranch, and what I predict would be the profit margin when we're done. There's a step-by-step plan all written out." He stood. "A little light reading while you're resting after therapy. Provided you don't run Ms. Upton off for good."

Win left without saying anything else. After his father's surgery, he'd come to realize that the ranch meant something to him, and so did his crusty father, but Win wasn't going to bang his head against the wall forever, either. He was building a future for himself and his family. If it meant quitting the ranch as soon as the loan was approved and devoting himself to getting the lavender farm off the ground, he would do that. He could get Jenny up and running, then find something else for himself.

He was a rancher. He would stay a rancher. But Jenny came first.

* * *

Jenny kept watch as she always did during the farmers' market for Win to arrive. He'd said he would be early because the Realtor wanted to meet up with them with a counteroffer and was coming to the market anyway.

She spotted him a few seconds later, walking that sexy cowboy stroll down the middle of Main Street, which was shut down to traffic on Monday nights.

She could watch him forever, how his narrow hips moved, how his strong, muscular thighs filled out his Wranglers, how his chest looked without his Western shirt, all broad and strong and kissable. And when he turned around—oh, my, what a sight he was, too.

"You're drooling."

Jenny jerked up at the sound of her sister-in-law's voice. Annie laughed.

"I wasn't drooling," Jenny said.

"He is one nice specimen of maleness," Annie said, as Win neared the booth. "Not as nice as my particular specimen, but close."

Jenny elbowed her, thinking Win was probably close enough to hear their conversation. His grin should've been enough of a clue, but when he grabbed her and bent her over for a kiss, she knew for sure he'd heard, and his ego was happy about it.

"Don't go getting all cocky now, husband,"

Jenny said pertly, which made him laugh. Annie joined in.

"Where's the baby?" Win asked Annie.

"At home with the grandparents for a couple of hours. I had cabin fever."

From across the way Mitch waved to her, calling her over to the honey booth.

"She looks good for having given birth three weeks ago," Jenny said.

Win nodded, then eyed her abdomen. "You've got a little bit of a swell now. I like it."

"Wait until I can't even tie my own shoelaces."

"I'm lookin' forward to it, you hot mama, you."

They'd definitely found accord the past couple of weeks, and a voracious desire for each other that he'd finally stopped worrying about.

"How'd it go with your dad?" she asked after she pocketed cash for a bouquet of daisies from a steady customer.

"No surprises."

Jenny had watched him struggle all week trying to put together a business plan for the ranch. She knew he'd been nervous about presenting it. "I'm so sorry."

"He didn't throw the notebook back at me, so maybe there's hope."

"Did Ms. Upton quit again?"

"Yep."

"Do you think your father is sweet on her?"

He looked surprised. "I have no idea. Seems doubtful to me. And there's no way she would return that. He's been nothing but ornery."

"Stranger things have happened. I wish I could drop in and see for myself."

The Realtor, Ellen Travis, approached, carrying a folder. "Well, they didn't budge," she said. "Actually, three would've made a new offer, but three won't budge. What do you want to do? You can come up a little and see if it flies."

Win didn't even hesitate. "Yeah, let's take it up some. We don't want to lose it."

We don't? The stunning words jammed Jenny's mind. "I don't think we should go much higher."

They wrote up another offer and signed it, but Jenny wasn't as thrilled about it as she was the first time. She had a feeling they were going to go round and round for so long it would be too late for a crop next year.

"What's wrong?" Win asked after Ellen left.

"Nothing."

He just looked at her.

"I don't like dickering," she said. "Everyone knows that about me. I set a fair price here at the market and that's that. I sell out every week, so apparently no one is offended by my policy. This business with the farm isn't sitting well with me."

"As Ellen said before—six people, six opinions. In the end, they'll come around, Jen. I think they'll all want to be done with it before too long. I sure would. They won't play around forever."

The booth suddenly became a Ryder event, with all of the siblings showing up, Adam and Brody with dates, Vaughn and Karyn, and then Haley a minute later, although without a date.

Jenny had talked to Haley on the phone when she'd returned from Kentucky, but she hadn't seen her. Jenny had only learned that Clint's condition was worse than Haley had anticipated, but she hadn't said more than that. "What's the latest?" Jenny asked Haley.

"I've already taken my leave because the ranch house on the property he bought didn't have any furniture. So I've been decorating, plus getting specialized therapy equipment, stocking the pantry. All that stuff."

"Are you having fun decorating?"

"Are you kidding? With someone else's money? Heck, yeah."

"And you think you can handle being around Clint, touching him?"

"Heck, no." Haley laughed. "But I'm thirty-two years old, Jen. It's time I took some chances, don't you think?"

"I do."

"Even if I get my heart broken."

"Even if," Jenny said. "I could help shop, if you

want. I only work in the gardens in the morning. It's too hot in the afternoons now."

"I'll call you." She waved at someone at a distance. "It'll be fun."

Since Jenny knew exactly how it felt to love someone who didn't love her back, she worried for Haley. But as Jenny wouldn't trade her situation with Win for anything, she also had hope for her sister, too.

Maybe the Ryder girls were just made that way—to love more than they were loved. Somebody had to, didn't they? It couldn't be fifty-fifty.

She studied Win as he stood in the group with her siblings. He held his own with them, was an equal, and she was glad of that. His father had held him back for years, but no one blamed Win for that. He'd matured into a likeable, strong man.

She was proud of him. Proud to be married to him.

The Ryder clan helped break down the booth at seven o'clock. Mitch and Annie followed them back to the farm and helped unload everything then left to pick up their sons from the doting grandparents.

Win and Jenny settled in for the evening, relaxing on the front porch for a while then getting into bed before the sun fully set. Neither of them instigated sex, neither fell asleep. She felt her husband's restlessness and finally rolled to face him.

"What's on your mind?" she asked.

He didn't say anything for a few long seconds. Worry began to seep into her thoughts, then he said, "I'm thinking about my father. He'll never change. I'm not sure I can accept that anymore."

Jenny heard resignation in his voice. He shouldn't have to live like that. He had enough on his plate with her, the lavender farm and the baby.

She curled closer, wrapping her arms around him. He tensed up for a moment, worrying her, then he relaxed. After a while she rolled over and spooned with him. His hand curved protectively over her belly—the reason for their marriage.

And as hard as it was to admit—the only reason.

Chapter Fifteen

Two weeks passed before the Realtor heard back from the heirs. Two weeks of Jenny poring over her paperwork, talking the business plan through again with Vaughn and generally fretting. She was almost to the end of her first trimester. The morning sickness was gone. Her energy had returned in full force.

And Win was more and more unhappy.

She didn't know how to help him. She'd started getting up early to make him breakfast, sending him off with a smile that turned into a frown as soon as he disappeared from sight. It wasn't what she'd come to expect from him. He'd always been so even-keeled and genial, easy to be around. He'd made her laugh, teased her into bed, was generous to her.

Now he didn't seem to have any energy or enthusiasm, as if their roles had reversed at the trimester mark. She could only guess why, because he sure wasn't confiding in her.

Since the beginning of their relationship years ago he'd shared his thoughts with her, probably because she was "safe," as she'd said to him. Who would she tell? And now he'd clammed up, when she was safer than ever, as far as she was concerned. She was his wife, which implied a contract of confidentiality between them.

So why don't you just ask him?

Because maybe I don't want the answers.

For now Jenny let go of the worry and enjoyed the farmers' market, as usual. It was peak season for all the growers, with produce galore. They were at seventeen booths, the most for the summer, and not only townspeople but tourists came to shop. The music this week was provided by a barbershop quartet who sang not the old traditional tunes but more current music, drawing in the younger crowd. Only six weeks were left until the end of the market season. By then Jenny would be seventeen weeks along. Her job at the farm wouldn't end because Annie grew and sold her produce year-round. Jenny was looking forward to cooler afternoons, however.

The Realtor arrived before Win. "They're a little closer," Ellen said. "Are we waiting for Win?"

"No." Jenny put out her hand for the folder. The number was closer but still above what Jenny thought it was worth. And she feared Win would say yes.

"Ellen, I need a favor from you," Jenny said.

"What's that?"

"I want you to take the papers and leave. I don't want to share them with Win, not yet."

Ellen shook her head. "I'm sorry, Jenny, but—"

"Please. He's going to agree to this price. I know he is. I don't want to."

"I can't. Not because I don't want to, but he already knows, Jenny. I talked to him a while ago. And you're right—he wants to accept."

"I quit!"

Win stepped aside as Ms. Upton stormed past him. Four weeks of therapy, four weeks of her quitting. It must be some kind of record, Win decided. But Haley was right. The woman had been able to get Shep to do the work, motivating him with insults and threats most of the time, but getting the job done. They could cut back on the therapy to three days a week now, his progress had been that good. He was still reluctantly using a cane, but Win figured that would be tossed soon.

"See you tomorrow," Win called after her.

For the first time ever, Ms. Upton turned around and smiled at him. Apparently she was enjoying the game herself. Had Jenny been right? Was his father sweet on the woman, and she on him? Win wasn't sure that stranger things had ever happened.

He walked toward the den, grateful Rose had gone shopping. He spotted his father at the window, watching Ms. Upton drive away.

So there *was* something between them. Would it soften the man? If she didn't return the feelings, would he turn into even more of an ogre?

"Dad."

He turned slowly, keeping his balance. "What?"

Win moved forward and passed his father a folded sheet of paper—his resignation. "I'm giving you a month's notice. We should be finished with escrow about then, and you'll be through the worst of the season's work."

No emotion crossed the man's face. He took the letter, scanned it then tossed it onto the coffee table. "Been thinking about this since our last conversation," his father said. "If you want to buy into the ranch now and be a partner, you'll inherit it—you and Rose—when I'm gone."

The offer stunned Win. It was a concession of sorts, but it wasn't enough. "No, thanks. You owe me already. Maybe if you'd trade what you've been underpaying me all these years..."

"I'm not changin' the offer."

"Then I'm not taking back my resignation. I'll go where I'm needed. And wanted."

"So, given the choice of this ranch with its family history or a lavender farm, you choose the farm?" his father asked.

"I choose my wife. My pregnant wife, who holds my future in her hands and her womb. Yes, I choose Jenny." It was where he belonged. "It's her dream. Maybe you don't remember having dreams. I do. It's hard when they die. I don't want her to go through that."

"If you go, you can't come back."

"No surprise there." Win left, not looking back, figuratively or literally, careful not to slam the front door on his way out. He waited for the relief to hit him, but it didn't, just a heavy ache in the middle of his chest. After seeing how the Ryder family lived and loved, and wanting that kind of family life for himself, he knew he had to sever all ties. Except with his sister, of course, although maybe that relationship would be hard to maintain in the end.

Win climbed into his truck and headed for the farmers' market and his wife. He shut down his emotions. Whatever small hope he'd had that his father would react differently fizzled and died, leaving an open wound that would need to heal from the inside out.

As he walked toward Jenny's booth, he tried to relax, to smile, to be excited about the new counteroffer on the land, which was probably the best they were going to get.

But the look on Jenny's face, the searching, seeking, tender look she gave him struck hard and fast. He reached the booth, told her he'd be back in a few minutes then kept walking to get his dinner. By the time he'd eaten and gone back, he'd found a sense of equilibrium again.

He pulled her into his arms for a hug, placed his hand on her abdomen for a moment then gave her a brief kiss.

She framed his face with her hands. "What's going on?"

He stepped back. "Long day. Have you seen Ellen?"

"She was here, then she got a call and had to leave. She said she'd catch up with us tomorrow."

"Did she show you the offer?"

Jenny nodded.

"What'd you think?" he asked.

"Still too high."

"I don't agree. We should accept it."

They couldn't continue the conversation. The event was winding down and people stopped by to pick up items Jenny had put aside for them, and then she did some trading with other sellers.

They broke down the booth and drove home in silence, as if each knew what the other was going to say. It wasn't until they got inside the house that Jenny finally spoke. They faced each other in the kitchen.

"You had no right telling Ellen we would accept the offer, Win."

"You would hang on forever, trying to save a few thousand dollars."

"More than a few. We need to agree on a price not just because *you* think it's right. It's a business decision." She stood her ground, her fists on her hips.

"It's the best we're going to do. We'll sign the papers tomorrow and get on with our lives."

"You won't even listen," she said, her voice shaking.

"What's your problem? It's your dream, Jen. It's what you want. Why are you angry?"

"Because you totally left me out of the loop, out of the decision. I'm not just your wife. I'm your partner." She seemed to want to say more, but left the room instead.

He heard the screen door slam as she went out of the house. After a minute, he poured two glasses of lemonade and carried them outside onto the porch. She wasn't there, however. He set down the glasses and went in search of her, finding her vigorously tilling soil in one of the high tunnel greenhouses.

"I know you don't want the farm," she said, not looking at him. "If you're doing this for me and it bombs, you'll resent me for an action *you* took. I will always be the bad guy."

"No, I won't. And you shouldn't worry so much. I'll take care of us. All three of us. I know what my job is, Jen. You'll be provided for."

She threw up her hands. "I don't want to be provided for. I want to work side by side with you, to be your partner, not some albatross around your neck. You didn't have a choice but to marry me. At least include me in the other important decisions."

He didn't know what to say to that. She was right. Four years ago he'd married her knowing it wasn't a choice but a necessity. She'd been only eighteen years old, was naive in the ways of the world. He'd gotten her pregnant. That time was his fault. He'd known better, should have been more conscientious about birth control.

And maybe he hadn't officially made a choice this time, either, to stay with her, to acknowledge their child, but he didn't regret it. She didn't seem to realize that.

He reached for her hands. "Choice or not, Jen, I'm glad to be married to you."

Her chin went up a notch or two. "You took

way too long to say that, Win. Way too long." She breezed past him.

He wasn't sure of his welcome in their bed later. She was already curled up under the sheet, her back to the bedroom door. He undressed and climbed in behind her, wondering if she was going to order him out. Well, he wasn't going anywhere, so she'd better not try—

She rolled over. He didn't see anger, just distress.

"I hate fighting with you," she said, laying a hand against his face.

"Me, too."

"I know you'll take care of us," she said, her voice shaky. "But you need to understand that you're not in this alone."

"I watched my father rule the roost, having total control over my mother and my siblings and me. It's not always easy breaking our examples, but I'm trying."

Except he still wasn't being honest with her. He hadn't told her he'd quit his job just when he'd come to realize how much it meant to him, that they *had to* make the lavender farm work. She would worry too much. He'd get a part-time job, work faster on the property, have it ready to go for the first planting.

He would make her dream come true, come hell or high water.

She came closer and kissed him. He reached for her, holding tight, kissing her hard and deep, feeling her answering need. He slid his hand down her, cupped her abdomen, a firm swell now.

Win threw back the sheets and pressed his lips to that little baby bump. He didn't want his child to grow up amid arguments and tension, as he had.

"Have you felt the baby kicking yet?" he asked.

"No." She ran her fingers through his hair. "I'm anxious for that."

"Me, too." He moved up so he could kiss her again. "Are we okay, wife?"

She hesitated a beat. "Yes."

Win felt a need to make love to her slowly and tenderly. There was a fragility about her tonight even as she'd been strong, too, in her demands for a partnership, for joint decisions. It was that inner strength that would make her succeed with her farm.

But enough of that. This was a time for rediscovery, for forging a new path with her, for showing her how much she mattered. He took his time, building slowly but inevitably toward giving her satisfaction, just her, no matter how much she begged him to come inside her. He felt a freedom with her he hadn't before. Maybe starting today he would become the man he'd always wanted to be.

Whatever the reason, he would cherish the memories they were making this night and carry them forever.

Chapter Sixteen

Jenny had never been to Morgan Ranch before. After talking with Rose, she timed her visit for when she knew Win would be far from the house. Jenny wouldn't be welcome. She knew that, but she had something to say to her father-in-law.

Morgan Ranch was her husband's past and his future. Except for the difficulty dealing day-to-day with his father, Win loved his work, and he was hurting from his father's rejection of Win's plans for the ranch's future. Even at the breakfast table that morning, deep down pain registered in his eyes and his posture, as well as his almost desperate kiss goodbye. She'd made up her mind then and there to do something about it.

Her father and her brother Mitch had argued about modernizing, too, and they'd managed to work things out between them. So she would intervene with Win's father, try to get him to see the light, that planning for the future was critical to continuing the tradition of Morgan Ranch. If he tossed her right out the door, so be it. She needed to try.

Rose let her in and pointed her toward the room where Jenny could find Shep. The house was gloomy—wood paneling, deep red curtains, old furnishings. Dark, all of it. *And oppressive,* Jenny thought. A little paint and the curtains open to the daylight would lighten things up considerably. She wondered how Rose dealt with it day in and day out.

She was curious about which room was Win's, and if she could pick it out as his, but she didn't get the opportunity to look. Every door down the hallway was shut except the one to the den.

She found Shep riding a stationary bike and watching the news.

"Good morning, Dad Morgan," Jenny said too enthusiastically.

He gave her a look. "Wondered how long it would take for you to show up. Come beggin' for your husband's job, did you?"

Staggered by his words, Jenny grabbed the nearest chair. She looked at the floor, trying to hide her expression from him as her world spun. Win had been fired? And he hadn't told her?

"Actually, sir," she said, pulling herself together. "I came just to visit you."

His mouth tipped up on one side. "Interestin' timing, I'd say."

Jenny sat in the chair, not waiting for him to invite her. "We haven't had a chance to get to know each other."

"I don't figure our paths will cross a whole lot, 'specially now. You don't live on the property, after all."

"Would you like us to?"

His brows went up at that. "You thinkin' maybe the Morgans could turn into the Ryders, create a family compound or something with communal meals and happy holidays?"

"Everything is possible. People just have to be willing to try." Jenny's racing heart began to slow. Win had been fired and hadn't told her. She couldn't reconcile that in her mind. No wonder he'd wanted to sign the real estate papers last night. He wanted to rush it through before the bank found out he wasn't employed anymore.

Shep continued to pedal. "Since I offered him the chance to become a partner and ultimately my heir and he turned it down, I don't see that happening, do you? And he did it all for you, a silly girl who got herself pregnant twice." He snorted. "You stole my son, destroyed his heritage, for a damn *lavender* farm."

As shock layered upon shock, one fact sang out to Jenny. Win hadn't been fired. He'd resigned, and he'd done it for her, sacrificed his rightful place for *her*.

Guilt and regret opened up inside her, a huge chasm of painful acknowledgement. She didn't deserve him. They hadn't had a real marriage but had played at it, not being honest with each other. She hadn't been a good wife, hadn't shown him enough gratitude. She'd argued with him just last night, wanting control for herself, when he was the one doing all the giving.

Worst of all, she hadn't told him how much she loved him. Maybe that would make a difference to him. She'd been holding back her fear of rejection so long and so hard, as well as her walled-off grief over her miscarriage, a grief she'd never shared with him. And he was such a good man, the kind who stayed. The problem was, she still wanted him to stay for the right reasons.

She didn't want him giving up his place at the ranch so that she could make them go broke creating a lavender farm, the pipe dream of a girl, not the realistic goal of a wife and soon-to-be mother.

"Got you thinkin', huh?" Shep said, breaking into her thoughts, looking smug.

"It seems to me," she said, standing, "that it's up to you to make the change, not him. If you could've seen him while you were in surgery, you wouldn't question his love for you, even if you've done everything you could to make yourself almost impossible to love. He's a good man. The best. But *he* made himself that way, not you. If you want to rescue your relationship, if you want the only son you didn't drive away to come back and work this ranch with you, you'll find a way to make it happen."

She started to leave then turned around. "You keep this up and you won't get to know your grandchild, either. I had a gruff, ornery grandfather like you. I'm sure you knew him. He also didn't let anyone tell him what to do or how to live, but somehow he still managed to have the love and respect of his children and grandchildren. It can be done. Ever heard of the word *compromise?*"

Shep's voice was harsh. "Win's as stubborn as me, you know, girl, just in a quieter way. He wouldn't come back."

"Try him." Jenny had done all she could do. Win was probably going to be furious at her for going behind his back, but she knew what it meant to have family on your side. She wanted her child to know all his grandparents. She wanted her husband to be doing the work he loved.

Her motives were pure. Would Win see it that way?

They were supposed to meet at the Realtor's office after he was done at the ranch. Would Shep mention that Jenny had been to see him? Would Win already be angry about that?

Angry enough to insist on that marriage of convenience she'd told him she didn't want?

No. She would fight for him. He was the only one who mattered.

Win walked to his truck after a long day working at the ranch. He snatched a piece of paper from under his windshield wiper, having spotted it as he climbed into his vehicle.

"Dad wants to see you," the note read.

That couldn't be good—and he had other things to do, so he ignored it and drove off. Jenny was sitting on a bench outside the Realtor's office when he arrived. She looked nervous or wary or something.

"Ready?" he asked.

"No."

His shoulders dropped. "I don't want to argue in public with you, Jen. People will stare."

"There's no need to argue, Win. It's simple. I'm not signing the papers, not for the farmland and not for the loan. I don't want to do it anymore. I've come to realize it's too much to take on."

He didn't buy that for a second. It was all she'd wanted since before she'd graduated and come home. She'd put all that effort into coming up with a plan, had been excited and eager to accomplish her vision, had been so devastated at being denied the loan that she'd ended up having sex with him in the truck, in the rain—and that had created a baby. And this situation they were in.

Her desire for the farm couldn't change overnight, so what had caused this?

"Did my father call you?" he asked.

"No." She shifted. "But I went to visit him."

There was his answer. His father had gotten to her. "Why?"

"I was making an effort to reach out to him, to start building a family relationship. I thought it would be important, not just to you, but our baby. Instead I found out you'd resigned. You can't resign, Win."

"I'll do whatever I think is right for us, and for myself. I'm done with him."

"Okay. Well, in that same sense, I'm done with the lavender farm. Where does that leave us?"

He still didn't believe her. His father had manipulated her. She'd decided to sacrifice her dream farm for him, so that he could inherit the ranch someday. He didn't want it, not with his father's strings attached.

"Let's go sign the papers, Jen."

"I already told Ellen we weren't going to counteroffer. Win, we would never make a success financially of it. I imagine you've seen that yourself but didn't want to disappoint me. Thank you, but let's set the dream free."

So, she didn't have faith in him to help her pull it off. That's what it boiled down to for him.

"I'll see you at home later," he said, done talking about it. He got into his truck and took off.

There was something she was leaving out, he decided as he headed to the grove—their grove—to think. He didn't know what it was, but it was important.

And their marriage depended on her telling him, whatever it was, or his figuring it out.

She wouldn't give up her dream out of fear that she wouldn't succeed—she had too much confidence in herself for that.

So why was she doing it? Once he knew that, they would move forward.

Jenny didn't know where to go. If she went to the farm she'd be alone. She didn't want to be alone. If she went to the homestead, her mother would give her that look that said, "Talk to me."

She didn't want her mother to have that much information.

So Jenny headed for Annie and Mitch's house. She could use the excuse of wanting to hold the baby then ease into talking about her dilemma. Maybe.

Jenny pulled into the driveway in front of Mitch and Annie's house. Annie was on the porch nursing Jamie.

"Pull up a rocker," Annie said. "Mitch and Austin just left for town. They're going to the movies."

"Babies grow so fast," Jenny said, cupping the back of Jamie's head for a moment.

"They do. He's sleeping through the night. It's lovely to get a full eight hours rest, although Mitch has been the one to get out of bed, change his diaper and pass him off to me. I knew he'd be hands-on, but I hadn't realized how much." She turned a steady gaze on Jenny as she took a seat in the next chair. "I'm guessing Win will be the same."

"I know he'll be as different from his father as he can manage," Jenny said. She drew a deep, shaky breath. "I love him so much, Annie. And I can't tell him."

Annie barely reacted to what should have surprised her. "Well, first of all, I'm sure he must see that, since all the rest of us do. Second, why can't you tell him?"

"I'm afraid I'll say it and he won't say it back."

Annie closed her eyes for a few seconds, smiling. "Mitch told me he loved me every day for more than a month before I believed him. Before I allowed myself to believe him. I was so scared to tell him I loved him, too."

"Why?"

"Because then we would have to move to the next level."

"Marriage?"

"No, although that worried me. I'd already failed once, and I'd decided I wouldn't get involved with a man again until Austin was grown so that he wouldn't be hurt, either."

Annie toed the rocker steadily. "No, the next level for me was total honesty. I had to share my fears, my failures and my disappointments. I wanted him to see me as this perfect woman he'd conjured up in his mind, and if I shared all that with him, he would see I really wasn't perfect."

"And it didn't matter, because you were—are—perfect for him."

"Yes."

"You have a good marriage. A solid one."

"Because I stopped worrying about what he might think and just trusted him to accept me as I was. Plus you've seen him with Austin. Mitch won't hurt either of us." She brought Jamie up to her shoulder and rubbed his back. "Tell Win you love him, and whatever else is weighing on your mind. Trust him."

Trust him. She did trust him with physical and financial issues, but with her emotions? With the pain she'd held close to her heart for four years?

She would do it tonight. She would rip off the bandage then deal with the aftermath.

Jenny drove home, anxious and fretful. She didn't attempt to make dinner because she couldn't possibly eat a bite, so she poured herself some iced tea and sat on the porch to wait for her husband to come home.

Chapter Seventeen

Win had barely settled in at the river when his phone rang. He eyed the number. It could be either his father or Rose. He didn't want to talk to either of them. He had to figure what to do next with his life, how to handle his marriage.

But as much as he tried, he couldn't just ignore the call.

"Win!" Rose shouted in the phone. "Dad's on his horse! He's off somewhere riding right now!"

A litany of choice words rolled off Win's tongue before he said, "Call—I don't know. Maybe call Ms. Upton. We can't call 911 until we know there's a need. I'm twenty minutes away."

He tossed the phone onto the passenger seat and flew down the back roads, reaching the ranch in record time.

"Your horse is saddled," Rose said as he zipped into the yard. "Carlos and the others are already out looking for him." She passed him a walkie-talkie then wrung her hands. "He has to be all right. He has to."

Dread settled in Win's gut. "He'll be okay," he said as much to himself as his sister. He checked on everyone's location then headed in a different direction, and the route that made the most sense to him, anyway.

He shouted over his shoulder, "Call Jen, will you? Tell her I won't be home for a while."

"Okay."

"What are you trying to prove, old man?" Win asked the open expanse in front of him. He used his walkie-talkie several times, hoping his father had taken his with him, but got no answer. Every once in a while, an echo of one of the ranch hands calling his father's name reached his ears but got no answering cry.

The only destination of importance on this particular route was the family graveyard. He didn't consider his father sentimental, but maybe he was feeling vulnerable now, not so invincible. The path got rocky toward the top of the hill. His horse could have slipped or something, his father not strong enough to hold tight with his legs the way he would normally.

"Dad!" he yelled as he started up the path. Again and again he called out. It would be dark before long. He wouldn't freeze, but if he had fallen and was unconscious or bleeding...

"Don't go there," Win muttered. "He's fine. He's just being ornery."

But if he'd done damage and had to go through surgery and rehab again? Win didn't want to think about it.

"Win? Over." Carlos shouted into his walkie-talkie.

"I'm here. Over."

"No sign of him or his horse on the northwest and northeast properties. Over."

"Thanks. I'm near the graveyard. Will let you know. Over."

"Ten-four."

Win scanned the horizon. If his father had been thrown from his horse, he wouldn't be alone. Zeke was too well trained for that. Seeing a riderless horse would be okay because it meant his father had to be nearby.

He rounded the hill and saw the horse first, then his father, sitting on a log. Win's tension should've lessened but didn't.

"You okay?" he asked, dismounting. His heart

thudded as he checked his father out visually, expecting obstinacy in return.

"Mostly."

"You fall?"

"Nope. Got down under my own steam. Can't get back on. Figured you'd find me sooner or later."

Win sat next to him. "You didn't take your walkie-talkie or phone?"

"Rose has the phone." He pointed. "Walkie-talkie's just over that rise. I dropped it when I got off Zeke, which was kind of a bumpy maneuver. I was gonna try to get it in a few minutes."

"Are you hurt? Should I send for help?"

"I think between us, we can manage to get me back on Zeke."

Win lifted his walkie-talkie. "Got him. We're at the graveyard. I don't think we'll need any help, so head on back before it gets dark. I'll call if I need you here. Over."

"*Dios mio,* thank you," Carlos answered. "Over."

"Why'd you do it, Dad?"

"Needed to know I could. And I had some things to think over. Don't need no lectures, either. I took it real easy gettin' here." He rubbed his thigh. "Hurts like it does after Ms. Uppity's done with me. I'll be fine."

Win angled his head toward his mother's headstone. "You been talkin' to Mom?"

"Yep."

"Did she answer?"

Shep sort of laughed. "Lorene, she gave me an earful, all right."

Win waited, hoping the conversation would continue. His father seemed mellow for the first time in, well, ever.

"I heard Jenny came to see you," Win said.

"You know that term *steel magnolia?*" Shep asked. "They coined it after her. She gave me hell in the softest, silkiest way a woman could. Threatened to keep my grandchild from me. Now, I know I got others, but since I've never seen any of 'em, this one would matter."

"You could see the others if you'd get in touch with your other sons."

"I don't need no reminders of what I should and shouldn't be doin', okay?"

"Okay. So is Jenny responsible for you being here today?"

"In a way. And Ms. Uppity."

"You like her." A statement, not a question.

"Don't know why, but I do. Maybe I'm just lonely. But I needed to talk to your mom about her, ask if it was okay if I went on a date."

"What'd Mom say?"

"What do you think?"

"I imagine she gave a thumbs-up."

"She said I was too young to be spendin' my

life alone. Hear that? Too young. Told you I wasn't decrepit."

"You're not looking young at the moment."

He groaned as he tried to move. "Not feelin' it right now either, but I will once I get back to the house and take a coupla aspirins."

Win didn't want the conversation to stop, but he knew they couldn't linger much longer. "Do you want to try to mount up? We're losing the light fast."

"Yeah. I sure don't like having to lean on you, son."

"Everyone needs a helping hand now and then. I didn't tell you before, but two of Jenny's brothers helped moved the herd the day you had your surgery. They volunteered. I didn't ask."

Shep seemed to take that in for a minute. "Jim Ryder's reached out to me before. I turned my back on him."

"Well, here's your chance to change that. Our families are connected now—for life. If you could see fit to smiling now and then, and accepting invitations, maybe you could share in all the big events. Maybe you could even host your own."

"Maybe. Maybe Ms. Uppity would help."

"I've seen the way she looks at you, Dad. She's not gonna turn you down."

His eyes lit up, then his face relaxed with relief. "Okay. Good."

They managed to get Shep back on his horse and set off for home, taking an easy pace, although Win caught him wincing a lot.

The first one to yell at him was Ms. Upton. "You fool. You damn fool. Get down off that creature and let me check you out, then I'm quitting. For good this time. I mean it."

"Ms. Uppity," Shep said, then stopped. "Frannie. I'd be mighty pleased if you'd let me take you to dinner one night soon."

Her mouth agape, she stared at him. "You're asking me on a date? In front of all these people? You figure that way I won't say no?"

"I'm hopin'."

Win looked at the grinning group, who hadn't moved an inch but stood there enjoying the floor show. Carlos and all the ranch hands exchanged humorous looks. Rose covered her mouth, her eyes twinkling. Jenny— Jenny was there? And her family. A herd of horses were in the yard. The Ryders had come to help search.

Win caught his father-in-law's gaze and nodded his thanks. Jim simply touched his hat, as if to say, "No thanks necessary. It's what we do for each other."

"All right. Yes," Ms. Upton said finally, and everyone cheered. "Let's get you in the house and see how much of my work you've undone."

"Win can help me to my room. Give us a few minutes, please. We've got business to attend to."

We do? Win asked silently, hoping his father had talked to his mother about more than just Ms. Upton.

Shep was helped off his horse, then Rose handed their father his cane. He leaned on it heavily. Win didn't touch him but was close enough to help should it be necessary. He glanced at Jenny, whose brow was furrowed and hands were clenched, so he stopped next to her for a minute.

"Thanks for enlisting the cavalry," he said.

"All I did was call. They came on their own."

He ran a finger down her tight jaw. "We have things to talk about, don't we?"

Her hesitance to answer cut into him. "Yes," she said.

"Good or bad?" He wanted to be prepared.

"I don't know. Could go either way, I guess."

That got him worrying a bit.

Win waited for his father to sit before he took a seat himself on the couch.

"Okay, here's the deal I made with your mom a little while ago," his father said. "You stay on here, I'll make you a partner, and I'll give you the back pay you think you deserve."

Win's blood sped through his body, pumping his heart hard and fast. "That I *do* deserve. As do the others."

"We'll figure something out for them. Your job will be to bring the ranch up to speed, modernize it as you called it."

"You'll include me in all of the decisions," Win said. "And my vote will carry weight."

His father nodded.

"You'll buy Rose a car of her own."

"You wanna wipe out my investments in the first week?" He held up his hands. "Okay, okay. So, where do you think you'll live?"

"I have to talk to my wife about that."

"You can pick a portion of land to build your own house."

"Jenny has land, too. We'll see." He stood. "What changed your mind?"

"Your wife, for one. But mostly I'm just tired of fightin' everybody and everything. Not being able to ride for a month showed me what my future could be. I didn't like it one bit. I probably won't do as much as I used to, but maybe I'll have Frannie with me and it won't be so hard. She keeps talkin' about all the traveling she plans to do. Can't say I'm ready for Paris, but maybe Yellowstone."

For the first time in Win's memory, he laughed at something his father said. "I'll send Ms. Upton in. I sure hope you didn't do any damage to yourself or have a setback that adds months to your recovery."

Win could hardly contain himself. He'd just

been given everything he'd asked for, *more* than he'd asked for.

Which begged the question of Jenny's lavender farm. It wasn't too late to sign the papers. He knew she'd been willing to sacrifice it, but now that their financial situation had changed, she could still do it.

When he reached the front yard he found her family gone.

"He's ready for you, Ms. Upton," Win said. "Rose, you and I can go car shopping tomorrow, if you want."

Rose leaped at him, giving him a big hug.

"Lots of things are going to change," Win said. "Lots."

Rose stepped aside and there stood Jenny, his beautiful wife, looking curious. "Shall we go home?" he said.

Soon they pulled into the farm's yard.

Hungry and dusty, they sat on the porch steps and faced each other.

Jenny hoped Win would speak first, because she had no idea how to start the important—no, critical—conversation.

"Partly because of you," Win said, beginning the discussion, "and partly because of his attraction to Ms. Upton, and partly because of his surgery, my father has seen the light."

"A strobe or a penlight?"

He smiled. "One of those Hollywood search-lights."

"That bright? You must be shocked and awed."

Win nodded. "To sum it up, he's making me a partner and giving me a real voice in the operation and modernization of the ranch. He wants me to choose a piece of property of my own for a house. He wants to be involved in our lives."

"And apparently he wants Ms. Upton."

"In a major way." He reached for Jenny's hand. "You can have your lavender farm."

It took her breath away hearing those words but also seeing the look in his eyes, his pride and satisfaction in being able to fulfill her dream. Except—

It was time to lie to him for the last time. Never again after this, but this was a good and important lie.

"I don't want to create the lavender farm anymore, Win. I told you that." She did want it—badly—but it wasn't her time. It was his. He deserved a normal life. They all did.

"That was before my father offered me a partnership. It'll still be a bit of a struggle financially, but we can do it. I'm sure of it."

"You're not hearing me, Win. I don't *want* it. My priorities have changed." She put a hand on her abdomen. "I don't think this is the time to be attempting something so challenging and potentially ruinous financially. When I came up with the idea I was in a different place than I am now. I'm okay with it, Win. Truly."

His eyes told the truth. He was relieved and grateful. She'd made the right decision.

"Later on, then," he said. "When the kids are in school."

"Kids? Plural?" It was his first mention of more, she realized.

"Do you only want the one?" he asked.

It was the opening she needed. Now or never. "Did you grieve after I miscarried?"

He backed away a little. His face became a mask like she'd never seen before, emotionless and cool.

"I mourned for years," she said when he didn't answer.

"You never cried. Not with me. You said things like, 'It was for the best.' I thought you were glad."

"I wanted that baby. And you." Tears stung her eyes. This time she would let them flow, let him see the truth. "When I lost the baby, I lost you, too. A double blow. I wanted to mourn with you, but I didn't know how. Didn't know if you felt the same or were just relieved to have the relationship end. I needed you. I didn't know how to tell you that."

The tears fell then, hot and salty, down her cheeks. When she finally looked at him, his eyes were shimmering wet, too.

"I thought you were glad," he whispered.

She shook her head as she started to sob. They reached for each other at the same time, clung together, grieved together for the first time after four years of holding back. The ache of loss engulfed them, but it was the only way they could heal.

"I put up walls so I wouldn't feel anything," he said. "I never dated. I couldn't. I was a married man."

"I tried to date," she said, resting her head on his shoulder, his arms around her. "I never slept with anyone. It was you. Always you. Only you."

"I love you," he said. "Always you. Only you."

"I love you, too." What a relief to say the words finally. "I love you with all my heart and all my soul."

"I love you more."

She laughed, the sound shaky and watery. "Why didn't you say so?"

"I didn't understand what love was, not really. I liked you. I wanted you. I even needed you. It wasn't until we thought you were miscarrying again—and I was afraid that would end our marriage for good if it happened—that I realized what I felt, had always felt, was love. But you'd miscarried right after we'd had sex and I lost you. The thought of losing you forever..." He shook his head. "I knew I would do everything and anything to keep you, wife."

"I'm not going anywhere, husband. Ever. We belong to each other."

Epilogue

"Merry Christmas, wife," Win said, handing Jenny a package with a big red bow.

Jenny basked in his love. They'd given each other gifts for months, whether for the real Christmas or birthdays or other occasions but always wrapped as Christmas presents. "It's March, husband."

"The biggest and best Christmas of all." He leaned over her hospital bed and kissed her, then the forehead of Elizabeth Ryder Morgan, born two hours earlier.

Jenny passed Beth to her daddy, got a lump in her throat at the tender way he looked at their daughter, then she opened the package and found a stack of paperwork.

"I'll sum it up," he said. "You and Annie are officially co-owners of Ryder-Morgan Farm, grower of organic produce, table flowers and lavender. Your signature is required about fifty times, then it's yours."

"Ours."

He met her gaze and smiled. They shared everything now—a daughter, land and their emotions. Neither held anything back.

"Sit in the rocker," she said. "Enjoy your daughter for a while. I'll doze, I think."

It didn't take any convincing. He settled in, and Jenny closed her eyes.

What an amazing few months they'd had, she thought as she drifted. Annie had offered to sell them half of her farm, realizing she wanted to be with her children as much as possible. She would be happy splitting her time there, especially with someone who understood her goals. Annie and Jenny could share the time and the work, a bonus for both of them.

Then Win suggested he and Jenny build their family home on her Ryder Ranch property. That way he could choose as his own the Morgan grazing land surrounding Annie's farm, which expanded that property, and Jenny could plant her lavender. It would be a much larger farm, open to the public now and then, a place to draw tourists but also the local townspeople for U-pick days, too, during berry season and Halloween—and lavender picking.

The Ryders and the Morgans were connected now. Even Win's father had warmed up. Maybe the word *mellow* couldn't be applied to him, but he was going and doing with Frannie, leaving Win to manage independently a lot. Win had come into his own.

As for Jenny, as long as she kept getting Christmas gifts with love and big red bows, she would be a happy woman.

* * * * *

REQUEST YOUR FREE BOOKS
2 FREE NOVELS PLUS 2 FREE GIFTS!

⊞ HARLEQUIN®

SPECIAL EDITION
Life, Love & Family

YES! Please send me 2 FREE Harlequin® Special Edition novels and my 2 FREE gifts (gifts are worth about $10). After receiving them, if I don't wish to receive any more books, I can return the shipping statement marked "cancel." If I don't cancel, I will receive 6 brand-new novels every month and be billed just $4.74 per book in the U.S. or $5.24 per book in Canada. That's a savings of at least 14% off the cover price! It's quite a bargain! Shipping and handling is just 50¢ per book in the U.S. and 75¢ per book in Canada.* I understand that accepting the 2 free books and gifts places me under no obligation to buy anything. I can always return a shipment and cancel at any time. Even if I never buy another book, the two free books and gifts are mine to keep forever.

235/335 HDN F45Y

Name	(PLEASE PRINT)

Address	Apt. #

City	State/Prov.	Zip/Postal Code

Signature (if under 18, a parent or guardian must sign)

Mail to the Harlequin® Reader Service:
IN U.S.A.: P.O. Box 1867, Buffalo, NY 14240-1867
IN CANADA: P.O. Box 609, Fort Erie, Ontario L2A 5X3

Want to try two free books from another line?
Call 1-800-873-8635 or visit www.ReaderService.com.

HSE11

*Romance is the last thing on new mother
~acey Fortune Jones's mind...until rancher Colton Foster
~omes along. Will love emerge where she least expects it?*

***

What are you thinking?" he asked.

She told herself to get over her self-consciousness. After all,
is was Colton. He might as well be one of her brothers. "If you
ust know, Mr. Nosy, I was thinking that you have the longest
~elashes I've ever seen on a man. A lot of women would give
~eir eyeteeth for your eyelashes."

Surprise flashed through his eyes and he laughed. It was a
~rong, masculine, happy sound that made her smile. "That's
~first."

"No one else has ever told you that?" she asked, and narrowed
~r eyes in disbelief. Although Colton wasn't one to talk about
~s romantic life, she knew he'd spent time with more than a
~oman or two.

He shrugged. "The ladies usually give me other kinds of
~mpliments," he said in a low voice.

Surprise and something else rushed through Stacey. She had
~ver thought of Colton in those terms, and she wasn't now, she
~ld herself. "What kinds of compliments?" she couldn't resist
~king.

"Oh, this and that."

Another nonanswer, she thought, her curiosity piqued.

The song drew to a close and the bandleader tapped on his

microphone. "Ladies and gentlemen, we have less than a minute left to this year. It's time for the countdown."

Stacey absently accepted a noisemaker from a server and looked around for her daughter. "I wonder if Piper is still with Mama," she murmured, and then caught sight of her mother holding a noisemaker for the baby.

"Five…four…three…two…one," the bandleader said. "Happy New Year!"

Stacey met Colton's gaze while many couples kissed to welcome the New Year, and she felt a twist of self-consciousness. Maybe a hug would do.

Colton gave a shrug. "May as well join the crowd," he said and lowered his head and kissed her. The sensation of the kiss sent a ripple of electricity throughout her body.

What in the world? she thought, staring up at him as he met her gaze.

"Happy New Year, Stacey."

***

Enjoy this sneak peek from
USA TODAY *bestselling author Leanne Banks's*
HAPPY NEW YEAR, BABY FORTUNE!,
the first book in
The Fortunes of Texas: Welcome to Horseback Hollow,
a brand-new six-book continuity
launching in January 2014!

HARLEQUIN®

SPECIAL EDITION

Life, Love and Family

Don't miss the final chapter of
THE CHERRY SISTERS trilogy
by reader-favorite author Lilian Darcy!

Gorgeous Joe Capelli is back from Hollywood!
Will a summer fling with former classmate
Mary Jane Cherry lead to something more?
All Mary Jane's ever wanted is a husband and family
As her old crush on Joe revives itself, dare she believe
that handsome, gorgeous Joe actually wants her,
too—and for more than just a steamy summer affair

**Find out in the new installment of Lilian Darcy's
THE CHERRY SISTERS miniseries!**

The Cherry Sisters: Three sisters return to their
childhood home in the mountains—and find the
love of a lifetime!

**Look for *IT BEGAN WITH A CRUSH* next month from
Harlequin Special Edition, wherever books are sold**

www.Harlequin.com

Love the Harlequin book you just read?

Your opinion matters.

Review this book on your favorite book site, review site, blog or your own social media properties and share your opinion with other readers!

Be sure to connect with us at:
Harlequin.com/Newsletters
Facebook.com/HarlequinBooks
Twitter.com/HarlequinBooks

HARLEQUIN®

A *Romance* FOR EVERY MOOD

Stay up-to-date on all your
romance-reading news with the
Harlequin Shopping Guide,
featuring bestselling authors, exciting new
miniseries, books to watch and more!

The newest issue will be delivered right to you
with our compliments! There are 4 each year.

Signing up is easy.

EMAIL

ShoppingGuide@Harlequin.ca

WRITE TO US

HARLEQUIN BOOKS
Attention: Customer Service Department
P.O. Box 9057, Buffalo, NY 14269-9057

OR PHONE

1-800-873-8635 in the United States
1-888-343-9777 in Canada

Please allow 4-6 weeks for delivery of the first issue by mail.

HSGSIGNU